THE
OVERLAND
ESCAPE
LEE RODDY

THE OVERLAND ESCAPE

LEE RODDY

BETHANY HOUSE PUBLISHERS
MINNEAPOLIS, MINNESOTA 55438
A Division of Bethany Fellowship, Inc.

Library of Congress Catalog Card Number 88–063471
ISBN 1–55661-026-2

Copyright © 1989
Lee Roddy
All Rights Reserved

Published by Bethany House Publishers
A Division of Bethany Fellowship, Inc.
6820 Auto Club Road, Minneapolis, Minnesota 55438

Printed in the United States of America

Library of Congress Cataloging-in-Publication Data

ISBN 1–55661-026-2

To
my wife Cicely
for always
believing in me

LEE RODDY is a bestselling author and motivational speaker. Many of his over 48 books, such as *Grizzly Adams*, *Jesus*, *The Lincoln Conspiracy*, the *D. J. Dillon Adventure Series*, and the *Ladd Family Adventures* have been bestsellers, television programs, book club selections or have received special recognition. All of his books support traditional moral, spiritual, and family values.

CONTENTS

AN
AMERICAN ADVENTURE
SERIES

CHAPTER
ONE
—

MOVED: NO FORWARDING ADDRESS

Hildy Corrigan knew something was wrong the moment she topped the last hill before reaching home that hot June afternoon. She stopped abruptly, the rocky ground hurting her bare feet.

Her cousin Ruby bumped into her from behind. "What's the matter, Hildy?" Ruby spoke with a definite mountaineer accent.

Hildy felt a strange, sickening sensation in her stomach. "I . . . don't know!" The slender twelve-year-old had only a trace of an accent, having vowed to become better educated than many of the mountain folk around her. Her brunette pigtails hung to the waist of her patched blue cotton dress.

Ruby, a year older and an inch taller, looked like a boy because of her short blond hair, faded blue overalls, and rumpled shirt. "I don't see nothin' exceptin' yore ol' house," she said.

Hildy frowned, staring through deep blue eyes at the rented Ozark Mountain log house where she had lived the past six months with her new stepmother, four younger sisters, and baby brother. Hildy's father was off somewhere looking for work, a difficult task in 1934, in the midst of the Great Depression.

"Something's wrong!" she exclaimed. "See? There's no smoke coming from the chimney. Molly should be fixing supper by now. And listen! No kids playing in the yard. But . . . oh!"

"What?"

"The windows! See?" Hildy pointed. "Come on!" She ran down the dirt trail toward the small house, which clung to the side of a heavily wooded ridge.

"What 'bout the windows?" Ruby asked, her bare feet running as fast as they could to catch up.

"The shades are gone. Something's happened. Something terrible!" The sick feeling in her stomach bordered on pain.

In moments, Hildy's long, gangly legs carried her wildly down the steep trail to the silent little shack with the vacant, staring windows. She veered slightly to miss the cedar tree that shaded the front of the house. Across the splintery wooden porch six sagging posts supported a galvanized-iron roof. Leaping up on the porch, Hildy jerked open the front door.

"Molly! I'm home!" she called. "Kids! It's me. And Ruby."

A single glance confirmed Hildy's fears. The house was empty. Hildy turned her anguished face to Ruby. "They're gone!"

"Cain't be. Try the other rooms."

The two girls rushed through the hollow, silent living room with its bare plank floor. The lean-to kitchen had been cleaned out. No furniture or belongings remained in the small bedroom Hildy had shared with her four sisters. The two iron beds were gone. The tiny closet was empty. So was the second bedroom, which her father and stepmother had shared with baby Joey.

The girls raced on through the house and out the front door. Hildy glanced wildly about. She had never known such agony of shock and surprise.

"Not a piece of furniture left, no clothes, nothing!" Hildy cried. "Not a sign of anybody, Ruby! Where could they be?"

Without waiting for an answer, Hildy sprinted around the back of the house with Ruby following close behind. She took the dirt path toward the outhouse, which leaned precariously. The door stood open, but only a yellow jacket buzzed around inside.

Without stopping, Hildy raced to the log barn, the only other outbuilding. It had partially collapsed, and the logs were hauled away when the Corrigans first moved in.

There was no sign of anyone in the barn. No cries of younger sisters or baby brother. No call by a concerned stepmother. Only a terrible, sad loneliness as the brooding hills rose silently above it all.

Hildy sprinted to the unpaved, rocky driveway to check for buggy or wagon tracks.

Ruby pointed at the dusty drive. "Thar! See the tracks? Hard rubber ones, not from a wagon."

Hildy's mouth felt as dry as the dust she stooped to examine. She looked at the tire tracks more closely. "Yeah. Only trucks have hard rubber tires. So somebody came and took everybody and everything away. But who's got a truck?"

"Yore new stepma's got a brother in Oklahoma, don't she? Maybe he's got a truck."

Hildy had seen only half a dozen cars in her life, and only one truck. Fighting a growing sense of panic that she'd been left behind, Hildy grasped at the hopeful thought. "Uncle Cecil! Maybe he came and took them all visiting someplace."

Ruby lowered her blond head and absently plucked at the snap on the front of her overalls. "That ain't likely, seein' as how they took ever' stick of furniture an' ever' stitch of clothes."

"Then, what else could it be?" she protested. "They wouldn't have just moved away and left me behind!"

Ruby's hazel eyes narrowed and she spoke softly. "Molly didn't much cotton to you, ye know."

"I know! I know! But I never did anything to her. We're a family. I mean, even if Molly can't ever replace Mom—not to me or any of the kids—we're still a family!"

"You'n her had some words 'bout that, didn't ye?"

Hildy waved an impatient hand. "A few, but no real arguments or anything."

"Went on fer 'bout six months, didn't it?" Ruby persisted.

"Well, yes, ever since she and Daddy got married. But we were trying to get along, especially with Daddy away!"

Ruby shrugged. "Molly prob'ly done went to find yore pa," she said bluntly.

"But he's looking for work someplace, and we don't even know where he is!"

"He sends money home, don't he?"

"Well, sure. But these are hard times, so he gets work where he can. He keeps moving from state to state."

"I don't want to hurt ye none, Hildy, but ye better face it. Yore stepma's done run off with the younger kids and left ye behind."

"No! She'd never do that!" Hildy shook her head so violently that her long twin braids swung wildly in the late afternoon air, slapping her in the face. "She wouldn't do that." All of a sudden a thought flashed into her mind and she snapped her fingers. "Hey, I know. Maybe they're visiting with the neighbors, or Granny. Come on, let's try the Naytons' place first."

Hildy knew that wasn't logical but fought to keep hope alive. She and her stepmother hadn't been close, but Hildy was very close to her sisters—Elizabeth, ten; Martha, seven; Sarah, five; and Iola, three. And everyone loved baby Joey, just thirteen months old.

Their mother had died when Joey was born. Hildy had taken care of her siblings until her father unexpectedly married a widow, Molly Murphy. And that's when their troubles began.

Now as Hildy and Ruby panted to the top of the ridge where the nearest neighbor lived, dusk slid silently across the treetops, settling darkly in the hollows and densely wooded areas. The Naytons' log house was nearly invisible in the shadows.

Suddenly two hounds, a bluetick and a redbone, charged out from under the high front porch, baying to announce the girls' arrival.

Sam Nayton stepped out on his rickety front porch and yelled at the dogs until they were silent. They retreated to the foot of the high wooden steps.

"Been 'spectin' ye, Hildy," Sam drawled. He glanced at Ruby but did not speak to her. His right cheek bulged from his usual wad of chewing tobacco. Pulling up the bib of his blue overalls, he fastened one strap while the girls approached.

Ruby and Hildy stopped at the bottom step, breathing hard. "We seen the truck drive off." The mountaineer spat tobacco at the redbone hound, and it dove under the porch.

"You did?" Hildy cried hopefully. "Who was it?"

A woman's voice came from inside the house. "I reco'nized the driver right enough. 'Twas yore stepma's no-'count brother, Cecil Holloway, from Oklahoma."

"Hesh up, ol' woman!" the man said without looking toward the house. He fastened the second overall strap and shifted the wad of chewing tobacco to the other cheek.

He looked down at Hildy, still ignoring Ruby. "Don't take no great head to figure out that yore stepma done skedaddled an' left ye behind like some worthless ol' houn' dawg. Likely gone to meet yore pa somewheres—maybe out Californy way."

Hildy sagged weakly on the bottom wooden step.

Again the woman's voice called from inside the house. "Hildy's still got her granny."

Hildy knew that ol' Miz Nayton was a gossip and enjoyed other people's hurts. Maybe that was because she was so crippled with arthritis that she couldn't leave her chair, and her bitterness made her talkative.

Her husband nodded. "My mizzus is right, Hildy. Ye got yore granny, which is more'n pore ol' Ruby's got in the way of kin." His words were meant to hurt Ruby.

Ruby instinctively started to yell, but Hildy grabbed her arm.

"Not now, Ruby!" Hildy raised her eyes to the man on the porch. "Which way did the truck go?"

The mountaineer pointed west. "Why, toward Oklahoma. Likely goin' d'rectly to that brother's place."

The woman's voice cackled from inside the darkened house. "That don't mean nothin'. They could've just struck out for yore granny's place. But that ain't likely, seein' as how she plumb despised Molly even more'n she did yore pa!"

Hildy turned toward Ruby. "Come on! Let's get to Granny's fast!"

"Y'all do that." The woman's voice was shrill. "Ghosts and haints'll git ye both if'n ye don't fly by the graveyard afore full dark!"

Hildy grabbed Ruby's arm again, knowing the taunting remark was for her cousin's benefit. Ruby was terribly superstitious, especially about graveyards.

Then Hildy turned and lifted her cotton dress above her knees so she could run easier through the gathering gloom. It wasn't fear of "haunts" and other imaginary dangers that drove Hildy. Her stomach knotted in fear because the unthinkable had happened. Even with Ruby right behind her, Hildy had never felt so scared and alone.

Only when Hildy developed a painful stitch in her side at the top of the final ridge did she pull up, panting, to rest a moment.

Ruby did the same, then spoke softly into the thickening twilight. "Hildy, I don't want to worry y'all no more'n ye are already, but yore ol' granny ain't likely to he'p ye none. She plumb hates yore daddy, an' always has! An' Granny don't like yore new stepma nor yore sisters nor brother, neither. Jist you."

"That's not true!"

"It's true, right enough. Ye know Molly or none of the kids'll be at yore granny's, don't ye?"

"Well, even if they're not, Granny's got to help me find them." Hildy stood and sprinted downhill toward her grandmother's home while the night closed blackly about her flying bare feet.

CHAPTER Two

GRANNY'S THREAT

Hildy saw the pale yellow light of the coal oil lamp in Granny Dunnigan's window and smelled the mixed aroma of wood-stove smoke and baking corn bread. But there was no sound of children and no sign of a truck in the unfenced back-yard.

"Granny!" Hildy called. "It's us!"

Hildy didn't want her to be alarmed at the sound of someone coming. Her superstitious grandmother had been known to shoot at sounds that startled her.

Granny came to the sagging front door, holding an oil lamp high. She raised her voice. "That you, Hildy?" Broken down by more than sixty years of hard work and bitter disappointments, the thin woman had stooped shoulders, and her mouth turned down in a perpetual frown. Her stern looks were made more so by her gray-streaked, mouse-colored hair parted severely in the middle and tied in a bun at the back.

"Yes, Granny! I'm with Ruby!"

Granny snorted her disapproval. She didn't like Ruby and made no attempt to hide her feelings. Granny was a sister to Ruby's grandmother. Although they lived within a few miles of each other, they hadn't spoken in years. However, Granny had other reasons for disliking Ruby.

"Where y'all been?" the old woman asked. Lowering the lamp, she pushed the squeaking door open with her foot.

"I spent the night with Ruby at her Grandma Skaggs' house." Hildy and Ruby stepped inside the familiar, small log home cramped with generations of clutter.

Granny snorted at the mention of her older sister. "She run ye two off with her sharp tongue?" the old woman asked, leading the way inside.

Hildy didn't answer. It was true that Ruby and her grandmother Skaggs had gotten into an argument this morning, and Ruby had stormed out, shouting that she was never coming back. But now Hildy's concern was to find her family.

Granny placed the lamp on a homemade table and sat down in a hickory rocker nearly as ancient as she was. "Sit a spell," she said, peering over the top of her small, wire-rimmed glasses.

The girls sat uneasily on two very old, homemade cane-bottom chairs. Grandpa Dunnigan, who had been dead for several years, had made all the furniture.

Hildy was glad Ruby wasn't saying anything. Hildy wanted time to figure out how to talk about Molly and the kids disappearing.

Hildy looked around absently at the walls papered with old newspapers. The pale yellow oil lamp illuminated the one large room where Hildy and Ruby sat facing Granny. Behind her was a small area, separated only by a curtain on a wire, where the old woman slept.

When Hildy stayed overnight, she slept in the loft directly overhead. A door at the far end of the big room led to a lean-to kitchen. The aroma of fresh corn bread made Hildy hungry.

"Granny, I got something to tell you," Hildy began.

"Somethin' turrible!" Ruby added.

"Hesh up, Ruby!" Granny snapped. "Hildy'll tell me all 'bout it." Granny's tongue was as sharp as her temper was short. Few people felt comfortable around her.

Hildy took a slow breath and looked thoughtfully at her

strong-willed grandmother. All but one of her seven children had died as infants or in early childhood. Only Hildy's mother, Granny's firstborn, had grown to her teens. Then she married and had six children. But finally Elizabeth died, giving life to baby Joey. So Granny Dunnigan was alone, bitter, and hard. Hildy remained her only source of hope or joy.

"Go on, Hildy!" Granny urged. Picking up her corncob pipe, she filled it with homegrown tobacco. Many of the older Ozark women smoked pipes.

"Well," Hildy went on, "when Ruby and I got to my house a while ago, Molly and the kids were gone."

Granny didn't answer. She struck a wooden match with a broken thumbnail and lit her pipe. As she puffed vigorously, the foul-smelling tobacco smoke drifted across her withered face toward Hildy.

Hildy wrinkled her nose in displeasure, then quickly filled in the details of discovering Molly's disappearance.

Granny rocked slowly in the scarred, black rocking chair and puffed her pipe in silence. When Hildy had finished, the old woman removed the pipe stem from between her false teeth. "Don't rightly surprise me none," she said at last. "Molly hated you 'cause you was more a ma to them young'uns than *she'll* ever be."

Hildy started to protest, but Granny held up her age-spotted hand for silence. "I jist took corn bread out of the oven. Ruby, go out and pull up the butter from the well. When ye come back we'll talk."

Granny set her pipe down in an old tin can and picked up the oil lamp. Silently, she stood and shuffled into the lean-to kitchen, leading the way for the girls. Granny set the light in the middle of a small table covered with a cracked oil cloth that had long ago lost its pattern.

Wordlessly, Ruby walked past the big cast-iron stove and out the back door. In a moment, Hildy heard the squeaking pulley at the well as Ruby pulled on the rope, bringing the butter and milk up from where they were kept cold just above the water-line.

"Granny, what should I do?" Hildy asked, fighting the panicky feeling inside.

The grandmother opened a cupboard beside the big wood-burning range. "I'm a-thinkin' on that. Set the table; after that we kin talk." She handed dishes down to Hildy.

Mechanically, Hildy set the table with the chipped, blue-rimmed dishes, but frustration churned within her slender body.

When Ruby returned, she carried two small lard buckets. One was filled with home-churned butter, and the other contained milk from Granny's only cow.

Granny took her time cutting the corn bread into squares, and Hildy wanted to scream. She *had* to find out what was going on. While the old woman placed one piece of corn bread on each of their plates, Ruby poured three glasses of milk.

As long as Hildy could remember, even when Grandpa Dunnigan was still alive, corn bread and milk was all that was ever served for supper.

"Ruby, you sit over there," Granny ordered, pointing to the chair on the opposite side of the table. "Hildy, take yore regular place here by me. I gave you the corner of that corn bread 'cause it's yore favorite piece. I'll say the blessin'."

Her prayer was short and routine. She never even said grace unless there was company. Granny regularly attended the small country church nearby, but her Christianity got all mixed up with her superstitious beliefs in spells and spirits. And at no time did she allow her religious beliefs to get in the way of her own strong opinions.

Finally, Granny was ready to talk. "Hildy, Lord knows I don't care none fer yore fiddle-footed pa. I kin never fergive him fer runnin' off with my only livin' daughter and marryin' without a proper ceremony. Justice of the Peace, indeed! And havin' you birthed in a sharecropper's shack, miles from anybody who cared!"

Hildy swallowed a bite of corn bread. "Granny, please don't start that again."

"Yore mother'd be alive today, I reckon, if'n Joe hadn't

dragged her over half the country, havin' all them kids, one after another. He jist let her git so sick and puny, no wonder she died young."

"Granny, please."

The old woman blew noisily through her open mouth. "'Sides, yore the only one looks like my Elizabeth," she said with a nod. T'other five young'uns take after their pa. I reckon that don't set none too good with Molly, neither. Every time she looked at you, she saw yore mother. So she found a way to get shed of ye, and she done it."

Hildy pulled back sharply as though she'd been slapped. "Granny, that's not true!"

"Molly ain't never a-comin' back, Hildy, and I say that's good riddance!"

"Then I'll go find her and the kids," Hildy shot back defiantly, raising her chin. She looked over at Ruby and nodded.

Granny's false teeth clicked as they did every time she became aggravated. "Now how's a half-growed girl like you a-goin' to do a thing like that?"

"I'll find a way."

Granny's voice softened. "Hildy, yore all I got left in this whole blessed world—leastwise all that means anythin' to me. So you'll stay with me, where ye belong."

"I don't want to stay here. I want to be with my family. Whatever's the matter between Molly and me, I'll fix it up with her."

The old woman's voice changed to almost a whine. "Don't ye love yore pore ol' granny?"

"Sure I do. But I love Daddy, and my sisters and baby brother, too. I belong with them."

"Ye love Molly?" the old woman demanded, her sharp dark eyes probing the girl's anguished face.

"I'm trying. But no matter what, we're a family, and we all belong together. Besides, after Mom died—when there was talk of splitting us up and parceling us out to friends and neighbors before we moved back here—I promised the kids that we'd stay together."

"That was before yore pa married that widder woman."

"It doesn't matter. I gave my word to all the kids." Hildy felt sick, realizing she might never see them again. She hurt with a pain so far down inside that she was sure nothing would reach it. Yet Granny didn't seem to notice.

Ruby had remained quiet, afraid to say anything for fear of further aggravating the old woman. But finally she spoke up. "I remember that time," she said, waving her fork in the air. "We was all a-sittin' at the table over to yore house, Hildy. The kids was cryin'—all of 'em—'cause they wanted their ma, and she was dead. They wanted their pa, too, and he was off somm'ers lookin' for work, and you was like the ma to them kids."

Granny glowered at Ruby for interfering, but the girl didn't seem to notice.

"It was little Sarah who cried the hardest," Ruby continued, "so ye took her in yore lap an' held her close. Ye said—I 'member it plain as day—ye said, 'Our daddy'll come back and take us off someplace where we'll never have to move agin. No more sharecroppers' cabins. No more tumbled-down shacks in the Ozarks. Californy, most likely. We'll git us a nice house—a big one. And there we'll all be together always. It'll be our *forever* home.' Them was yore exact words."

Hildy remembered, for all four sisters had repeated the words, almost as if they had a magic power. "Our *forever* home."

Ruby shifted uneasily under Granny's cold, disapproving stare. But Ruby had always been a rebel, so she added defiantly, "Hildy promised. She give her solemn word!"

"Ruby," Granny interrupted coldly, "ya clear the table and wash up them dishes. Hildy'n me'll talk some more in the other room."

The old woman took a second lamp down from a shelf, lit it with a kitchen match and carried the light into the big room. Setting the lamp on the table, she eased into her rocker again.

Hildy settled on the bare wooden floor at the old woman's feet. "Ruby's right, Granny. I promised the kids—"

"Sayin' to them kids that someday y'll all find yore 'forever home' was jist to make them feel good right then," Granny butted in.

"It wasn't that. I meant it. I still do. I've got to find them and then Daddy, and someday we'll have our home."

"Hildy, yore a-talkin' foolishness. Now, yore a-stayin' with me, and that's final!"

Hildy fought to control her anger and frustration. She wanted to jump up and run out into the night, to do something to ease the terrible ache and emptiness inside. But nobody defied Granny except Hildy's father, and Granny hated him fiercely. Hildy didn't want Granny to hate her.

She sat silently for a few moments until she regained control of her emotions. She could hear Ruby in the kitchen using the long-handled dipper to lift water from the bucket to the dishpan. Quietly, but with fierce determination, Hildy whispered, "Granny, I've just got to find them!"

The old woman leaned forward so suddenly that Hildy drew back. "Hildy, if'n ye run off, I'll have Vester find ye and bring ye back."

Hildy shivered at the name. Vester Hardesty was a no-account, superstitious mountaineer with a past so dark people only whispered about it. He said he made a living hunting and selling animal hides. Most people suspected he earned more selling illegal liquor, called moonshine. But there was something else about Vester that gave Hildy a nameless dread, a fear she couldn't place.

"Granny, you got no money to pay Vester."

Granny leaned back in her chair and laughed triumphantly. "Y'all might be plumb surprised what kind of cash money I kin lay my hands on if I was a-mind to. 'Sides, I'll tell 'im I'll put a spell on him if'n he don't fetch ye back."

"But I'll come back to visit!" Hildy protested. "I'll find Daddy and the kids—and Molly—and I'll come visit you sometimes. No matter where we live."

"Maybe ye would," Granny mused, "and maybe ye wouldn't. But mind what I say if ye ever think about leavin' here." She picked up her corncob pipe and relit it, puffing furiously.

Hildy felt as if she would burst. She had never known such

hurt since she'd kissed her mother's cold-as-marble forehead just before they closed the coffin.

As Granny's foul-smelling smoke filled the room, she removed her pipe and jabbed the stem toward Hildy. "Jist be thankful yore not like that woods colt cousin of yor'n! Ruby's not got nobody that cares fer her, even if'n she does live with her grandma, that miserable excuse of a sister I have!"

Hildy glanced uneasily toward the kitchen and whispered, "Granny, I wish you wouldn't call Ruby that."

"Call her what?"

"A woods colt. That hurts Ruby's feelings. Besides, it's not true. Her mother died when Ruby was a baby, and her daddy died before she was born."

Granny cackled with glee. "Is that what she done tol' ye, child?"

"Yes. He was poisoned with mustard gas in France during the war, but he didn't die until—"

"Believe Ruby's story if'n ye wants," Granny interrupted, waving her pipe, "but ever'body here'bouts knows the truth. Ruby's got no daddy—legal-like, anyways."

"Please, Granny. She'll hear you."

"Reckon she's heard worse. And the way she acts! Wearin' boys' clothes 'steada dresses."

"My mother used to say Ruby was just a tomboy, and she'll grow out of it."

Granny snorted. "She's a-growin', all right. Startin' to show signs of becomin' a young woman. Well, that's not rightly surprisin'. Why, come to think of it, I was married when I wasn't but 'bouta year older'n she is. Why, I had yore ma when I wasn't quite sixteen. But she weren't no woods colt."

Hildy had heard about Granny's ancestors coming to this hilly region more than a century ago. Lots of Scotch-Irish people had made Possum Hollow their home. And, like most Ozark people, Granny had countless relatives scattered throughout the mountains.

But after the war, the terrible Spanish influenza epidemic had claimed many. And those who escaped the flu died of old age, diphtheria, small pox, scarlet fever, or tuberculosis. Hildy's family, and Ruby, and her grandmother were the only relatives left.

Granny knocked the ashes from her pipe into the tin container by her chair. "Well, I hear Ruby a-puttin' them dishes in the cupboard. It's bedtime, I reckon. Now, Hildy, don't ye give another thought to yore no-good stepma and yore no-'count pa."

The girls silently climbed the ladder to the loft and undressed. Hildy's mind spun endlessly with a thousand thoughts. This was the worst day of her hard young life. She was so mixed up.

Ruby lay down on the corded bed with its sweet-smelling straw tick and goose-down pillows. She whispered, "Yore Granny's meaner'n her o'nery old sister."

"Oh, Ruby," Hildy moaned, "what'm I going to do?"

Granny blew out the lamp below, and soft shadows filled the log house. An owl called softly from outside, and far in the distance a hound started baying. The girls continued talking in whispers.

"I heerd what she said 'bout sendin' Vester after ye if'n ye leave," Ruby said. "He scares me—the way he looks at me, I mean. An' what people say he's done—turrible things!"

Granny's voice slapped through the darkness. "Y'all cut out the caterwaulin' and git some sleep!"

Both girls sighed. Ruby turned over to face the wall. Soon she was snoring softly.

But Hildy's mind remained active. Even if Molly had run off and left her behind, Hildy had to find her stepmother and straighten things out. Most of all, Hildy had to keep her promise to her four sisters and baby brother.

It was well after midnight when Hildy made a firm decision. "Tomorrow . . ." she whispered softly into the darkness; "tomorrow I'm going to start. I'll find them, and nothing or nobody's going to stop me!"

Chapter Three

ANOTHER TERRIBLE SHOCK

The next morning a rooster crowing in Granny's backyard woke Hildy. Opening her eyes, she stared at the low loft ceiling for a moment before she remembered where she was. Her resolution to find her family was immediately followed by doubt.

I can't go off and leave Granny, she thought. *If I go, she's got nobody left in all these hills except her sister, and they don't speak to each other.*

Ruby stirred and sat up in the bed the girls shared. "Ye look turrible, Hildy."

"I didn't get much sleep."

Ruby reached for her overalls. "What're ye goin' to do?" she asked.

Hildy hesitated. She heard the old woman shaking down the stove grate in the kitchen to remove the ashes. "I've got to find my family, but I don't know what to do about Granny," she answered. "I hate to leave her alone."

"She'n her sister don't give a hoot 'bout neither you nor me."

"Maybe you're right about Grandmother Skaggs. I know she doesn't care when or where you go. But I'm not so sure about my granny and me."

"If ye did leave, she'd send Vester after ye."

"I know."

"You scared?"

Hildy started to shake her head, then stopped and nodded. "Plenty!"

"Of Vester?"

"Him, too, but also . . . I was thinking. How can a girl my age go running around the countryside alone? It just isn't safe."

A slow grin moved across Ruby's face. She lowered her voice to be sure Granny couldn't overhear. "I know how," she whispered.

"You do?"

"Yeah. Soon's we kin git out of earshot, I'll tell ye."

A few minutes later, Granny told the girls to go wash up and bring in the butter from the well.

As the girls washed in a blue graniteware pan set on an old bench outside the house, Hildy urged her cousin to tell her how.

"Shhh! Wait'll we git to the well."

The girls dried their hands on a frayed towel and hurried on to the well. As they stepped up on the curbing, Hildy asked, "How can I stay safe if I go looking for my family?"

Ruby reached for the rope and began pulling it, hand over hand, from the dark recesses of the well. "Jist put on boys' clothes."

"I couldn't do that!"

"Why not?"

"I'm a girl. That's why."

"So'm I, but I wear boys' clothes all the time."

"But you're a tomboy."

"So?"

Hildy hesitated, critically considering her cousin's clothes. "I suppose that could work, except I don't have any boys' clothes."

"You kin use some of mine," Ruby answered, reaching out

to grasp the bucket as it cleared the top of the well.

For a long moment, Hildy considered the idea. Finally she nodded. "Vester *would* be looking for a girl, so boys' clothing *might* fool him."

Ruby grinned broadly. "Another thing. Ye won't be alone."

Hildy blinked in surprise. "I won't?"

"Nope. I'm a-comin' with ye."

Granny's shrill cry stopped further conversation. "Y'all a-goin' to talk all day? Git that butter in here so's we kin have breakfus'."

"Coming!" Hildy called.

Ruby unsnapped the lard pail of butter from the end of the well rope. "In boys' clothes, we can do some odd jobs in exchange for food on the road," she explained. She glanced down at the butter and handed the pail to Hildy. "Always surprises me how cold things keep down deep in the well. This butter's as hard as a rock."

The girls turned back toward the house, then stopped in surprise. A heavyset man in patched overalls, faded blue denim shirt, and a black slouch hat leaned against the corner of the back porch. A rabbit's foot dangled from the breast pocket of his overalls.

His pitted face, evidence that he had survived small pox, brightened with an evil grin. "Well, lookee here!" he said softly. "If'n it ain't my two favor-ite gals in the whole woods!"

"What do you want, Vester?" Hildy snapped.

The reddish beard split open as he smiled in mock surprise, baring his yellow teeth. "Ye don't sound real frien'ly, Hildy."

"She's not!" Ruby exclaimed, stepping forward to face the unwelcome visitor. "An' neither am I! So git outta the way 'fore we sic the dawgs on ye!"

"Now, Ruby," Vester mocked, "y'all know that Granny's ol' houn' done died quite a spell back."

He continued to lean against the porch, his dark eyes bright under heavy reddish-brown eyebrows. Reaching into his overall pants pocket, he removed a winter-stored apple and bit into it. A stream of juice ran unheeded down his whiskery chin.

Granny's voice shrilled from inside the house. "What's a-keepin' y'all? Git in here!"

Vester started at the old woman's words, his dark eyes darting toward the house. Slowly, he pushed himself away from the side of the porch and reached for the rabbit's foot he carried for good luck.

"Reckon I'll see y'all later," he said, chewing with his mouth open. "Got to go skin out some hides I took last night with my dawgs."

As he slowly moved off, Ruby shivered visibly. "He's the only person I ever knowed that makes me feel like I need a bath jist fer a-lookin' at him!"

"Me, too," Hildy answered softly, remembering some stories whispered about Vester. She carried the butter bucket toward the house. "I sure hope Granny doesn't really send him after us."

"Oh, she'd do that, right enough," Ruby whispered. "But we're a-goin' anyway, ain't we?"

For a second, Hildy's doubts returned. Then, remembering her family and her resolution in the night, she nodded. "I want to." She didn't mention the doubts or the sense of guilt that gripped her. "I have to!" she added.

Ruby opened the back door for Hildy to enter.

Hildy lowered her voice. "I figure Molly's gone to Uncle Cecil's in Oklahoma. If we can get there, I'm sure I can work things out with Molly so we can be a family again. But I still feel terrible about going off and leaving Granny."

"She don't keer nothin' 'bout ye!" Ruby whispered fiercely. "Deep down inside, she's plain o'nery an' selfish."

"She loves me and I love her!"

"She don't love nobody but herself!" Ruby cried hoarsely. "So let's start right after breakfast."

Granny had made buttermilk biscuits and white gravy seasoned with bacon drippings. The wonderful aroma filled the house, but both girls were so excited they barely noticed the food.

Granny's sharp old eyes missed nothing. After her hurried,

mumbled blessing, she asked suspiciously, "Now, what're y'all acookin' up that's so secret-like?"

A warm flush spread through Hildy's body. She didn't want to tell a lie, but neither could she tell what they were planning. Hildy cut off a piece of biscuit with her fork and sopped up some gravy before answering. "We just saw Vester Hardesty outside."

Granny's head snapped up, and her dark eyes glowed with anger. "He was here?"

Ruby nodded. "Rahtchere outside yore back door!"

Granny's eyes narrowed. "That means he was a-sneakin' around. He knows I don't allow that. But then I guess he knowed y'all was here, and he took a chance I wouldn't see 'im. I don't let him on this here place less'n I send fer 'im." She paused for a minute, then added, "He steals, ye know."

Hildy had heard that and worse. "Probably coming back from 'possum hunting," she said quickly, grateful for a chance to divert her grandmother's suspicions to Vester. "But I didn't see or hear his dogs."

"I swear he don't need dawgs," Granny replied. "More'n likely he picked up yore trail where you'uns come in last night."

Hildy cringed. "Is Vester that good at tracking?"

The old woman laughed. "He kin foller a shadder 'crost a winter-froze pond a week after it done melted in the spring thaw!"

Granny put down her fork and picked up a piece of biscuit with her gnarled, arthritic fingers. Wiping the last of the gravy from her plate, she said, "Hildy, if'n I was a mind to, I'da sent Vester to find yore no-'count pa. And Vester'd not come back without him, I promise ye."

Hildy welcomed an opportunity to change the subject and ask an important question. "Did Molly say where my daddy might be?"

Granny snorted. "He's in Californy. Workin' as one of them there cowboys, I heard tell."

Hildy had to be very careful what she said, but she also had to have some idea where to look for her father. "What part of Californy?"

"Don't rightly know. But yore stepma does. That's why she had her no-'count brother come git her and the other kids, a-leavin' you behind like ye was nothin'. But don't ye worry, none, Hildy. You'n me's a-goin' to git along jist fine!"

Hildy chose her words carefully. "Where . . . where does Cecil live?"

"Somewheres 'round Pontotoc County in southwest Oklahoma, I reckon. Works fer a cattleman near Blue River, I rec'lect Molly a-sayin' oncet. But you jist put that woman out of yore mind, Hildy. The very idee—a-runnin' off and a-leavin' ye like she done!"

After breakfast, the old woman ordered Ruby to do the dishes while Hildy helped put Granny's hair back in a bun. Hildy went to get the hairpins from the top of Granny's dresser, but when she reached to pick up the pins from between the big flowered ceramic pitcher and washbowl, she saw something in the partly opened drawer.

As Hildy slid the drawer open, she sucked in her breath so sharply that she almost choked. "My clothes and my only pair of shoes!" She quickly examined them. "Everything I own! But how? Why?"

Understanding hit hard. Angrily, Hildy shoved the drawer shut and raced into the kitchen where Ruby was dipping water from a pail into a dishpan. Granny scraped a plate into the slop bucket she always kept for her one butcher hog.

"Granny!" Hildy's voice came out shrill. "What're all my clothes doing here?"

The old woman didn't look up from her scraping. "Molly asked me to keep some of yore things here fer a spell," she said calmly.

Hildy could hardly keep from screaming. "Some of my things? Every last stitch I own is in your drawer! Molly didn't run off and leave me! You put her up to it, didn't you?"

"She don't love you, an' I do!" Granny protested. "'Sides, she's got them other young'uns to care fer. I'll treat ye better'n anybody ever done since yore pore ma died."

"But you lied, Granny!" Hildy's voice got higher and higher.

"You tricked me. You sent my family off without me. You did it on purpose!"

"Hildy, I done it fer you! Molly jist wanted an excuse. Otherwise, she wouldn'ta left without seein' ye, no matter what I said."

Hildy stared in angry, hurt disbelief. Then she turned and raced onto the back porch, fighting tears. In seconds she rushed back in with a tow sack, dashed to the dresser, and yanked open the drawer. Furiously, half-sobbing, she tossed her shoes and her few clothes into the sack.

"Hildy, what're ye a-doin'?" Granny asked shrilly.

Hildy didn't answer. Doubled over with hurt and pain, she swung the sack over her shoulder and staggered blindly toward the front door.

"Come back here!" Granny yelled.

Hildy barely heard her. Sobbing, she fled barefooted across the open yard, scattering frightened chickens. Then, hurrying past the pig pen, she climbed over the split-rail fence and headed up the steep side of the nearest mountain.

When she became winded, she collapsed on a log, her head in her hands. Her mind twisted like a summer cyclone, tearing her apart inside. *How could Granny do this? How could she? How? How?*

Suddenly a sound startled her. Hildy started to jump up, ready to run again if her grandmother had climbed the hill. Through bleary eyes, Hildy saw Ruby coming slowly toward her.

Ruby sat down beside her on the log and put an arm around Hildy's thin shoulders. "Yore Granny done a mean, low-down, rotten trick, Hildy."

Slowly, Hildy turned her tear-streaked face upward and set her jaw. "Yes, she did." She jumped up. "Ruby, I got no reason to stay here. Come on, let's go find my family."

SPUD

The two cousins ran through the woods to where Ruby had been living with her grandmother Skaggs. She wasn't home.

"It's jist as well," Ruby said as she dug into the tiny closet of her bedroom. "I wasn't a-lookin' forward to havin' a set-to with her 'bout takin' off like this."

Hildy watched as Ruby produced two old pairs of boys' overalls and blue homespun work shirts.

"Here," Ruby said, holding up the smaller pair. "Try these on."

Hildy stepped out of her plain cotton dress and stood there in her underwear.

Ruby laughed. "Molly musta made those out of an old flour sack."

"That's what she did."

"I kin still see the printin' on yore backside. Golden Best Flour, it says."

"Well, it's better than nothing," Hildy replied. Sitting on the edge of the high bed, she slid into the overalls and pulled them up over her underclothes.

Ruby reached down and turned up the cuffs for Hildy. "Well, they're a mite too big fer ye, but it's better'n havin' 'em fit too snug. Now, let's see how the shirt looks."

A moment later Hildy turned slowly for inspection. "What do you think? Can I pass for a boy?"

"Yep, 'cept fer them braids. Cain't have 'em. I'll git the scissors."

Hildy panicked. Her hands flew to the long brunette braids. "Do we have to?" she asked plaintively. "It took me years to grow these!"

"Cain't go around disguised as a boy with hair like that," Ruby told her firmly, returning with the scissors. "Sit down on that stool and let me see what I can do."

"No, Ruby, please," Hildy begged.

"Well . . ." Ruby said slowly. She screwed up her face as though trying to find an answer. Suddenly she clapped her hands together. "I know!" she exclaimed, grabbing a boy's cap from a nearby table. "Try this on."

Hildy understood and tucked her braids up under the cap. The gray golf-style cap with canvas visor felt strange, but a glance in the mirror showed Hildy that Ruby was right. If Vester came looking for them, both girls now could pass for boys.

"Looks good to me," Ruby decided, putting the scissors away.

Hildy took a deep breath and let it out in a slow, sad sigh. "We'd probably better wear our shoes in case we cut across some briars and brambles."

Both girls put on their four-eyelet oxford shoes they'd bought through the Sears and Roebuck catalog. Usually they only wore shoes on Sunday and in the winter.

Ruby found some cold corn bread and a couple of sweet potatoes in a cupboard. She stuffed them in a tow sack. "Ain't much," she said, turning to write a hurried note for her grandmother. "But I reckon it'll carry us 'til we find somethin' better."

The girls left the small log house with everything they owned slung over their shoulders in a couple of tow sacks. The sun was rising high when the two cousins started cutting through the woods toward the west. They stayed out of sight and off the main road so nobody would see them.

As they trudged along, the terrible reality of what had happened and what they were doing hit Hildy like a stabbing pain. She didn't know which hurt more—Molly's going off and leaving her behind or Granny's betrayal. Maybe it was the most recent hurt that made Hildy want to double over, holding her body with both hands to ease the pain.

Ruby seemed to sense her cousin's deep hurt. As they puffed up another steep hill, she tried to cheer Hildy. "Ye know, Hildy, if'n these here mountains could be straighted out so they didn't go up and down like they do, this county'd be bigger'n all Texas," she said, repeating the familiar Ozark joke.

Hildy didn't smile. She didn't even acknowledge that she had heard. Suddenly she stopped and held up her hand. "Listen!"

Both girls stood stock-still, their heads cocked to catch the sounds of the deep woods. In spite of how hard the climbing had been, they held their breath as best they could and listened.

"Somebody's a-singin'," Ruby whispered. "Boy or man, sounds like. Funny song. Ain't never heerd it afore."

Hildy nodded, catching some of the lyrics. "On the good ship, Lollipop. . . ."

She kept her voice low. "I heard those words once when I was over at the Naytons' place," she explained. "It was right after they got one of those new things that gets music right out of the air. What's it called?"

"Radio?"

"That's it. A radio. Got a big aerial wire strung from the house to the barn so they could get a signal all the way from Little Rock. Anyway, I heard that song on their radio."

"Yeah?"

"Yeah. A little girl movie star, name of Shirley Temple, sang it."

"Well, that ain't no little girl singin' now." Ruby stared into the distance. "That thar's a boy, but it ain't nobody's voice I reco'nize."

"We'd better hide," Hildy suggested.

The girls stepped off the narrow trail behind a scaly-bark hickory.

A squirrel in a nearby tree scolded noisily.

Hildy raised her hands to her lips. "Shhh! Let that singer go on by. Don't give us away."

Ruby giggled. "You shore sound tetched in the haid—a-talkin' to a squirrel."

"That boy's topping the rise," Hildy whispered. "I see his head." She studied the stranger carefully.

He was nice looking and about her height, strongly built with wide shoulders, narrow waist, and hands too big for his body. Even though it was summer, he wore a heavy aviator cap with goggles pushed up on top of his head. The straps hung loose below his chin.

Ruby giggled again. "What's them funny britches he's a-wearin'?"

Hildy stared at the strange navy blue serge pants that came just below the knee. "They're called knickers. I've seen pictures of them in the catalog. But I thought only little boys wore them."

"Maybe he's too broke to have long pants," Ruby said, still fighting the giggles. "Look at them funny stockings and them shoes he's a-wearin'!"

The boy's gray hosiery extended from his cuffed knees to his badly scuffed, high-topped leather shoes. The left sole had come loose. It was held in place with a stout string circling the top of the shoe and the sole. His little toe stuck out of a hole in the other shoe.

Hildy raised her eyes to the boy's face. He was ruddy with lots of freckles. Even his right hand, which held a stick over his shoulder, was covered with freckles. He shifted the stick slightly, and Hildy saw a huge blue and white polka dot handkerchief bulging at the end.

The squirrel continued chattering loudly, and the boy stopped singing and started looking up in the trees.

"He's a-lookin' fer that thar squirrel," Ruby said softly.

"Maybe he won't see us," Hildy whispered.

The boy turned and looked back the way he'd come. Then putting two fingers to his mouth, he whistled shrilly. "Lindy! Come on, boy!" he called.

"A dog!" Hildy's voice became a hoarse whisper. "He's calling a dog."

The girls looked at each other in dismay. The dog was sure to discover them. And then what? All their plans could be ruined before they barely got started.

Suddenly the dog bounded over the top of the hill and thrust a square muzzle against the boy's outstretched hands. Hildy didn't know much about dogs except hounds, and this wasn't a hound. It was a medium-sized animal with wiry, short black and tan hair. His tail had been cut off about six inches from his sturdy body, and he had no collar.

The boy straightened and pointed in the general direction of the girls. "Lindy, go find that squirrel. Maybe I can knock him out of the tree with a rock, and we'll roast him for dinner."

"Oh no!" Hildy's voice was a croak. "He'll find us for sure now."

Ruby squinted thoughtfully as the boy approached, the dog running ahead of him. "I'm bigger'n he is. I can whup him easy and run him off."

Hildy started to protest, but Ruby quickly stepped out of the brush, right into the path of the on-rushing dog.

Instantly, he slid to a halt. Dropping his head to protect his throat, he began walking stiff-legged toward Ruby.

Hildy heard a low growl. She reached down, picked up a small limb, and stepped out beside Ruby.

The dog kept coming, every ounce of his body threatening the two strangers before him.

Hildy raised the stick, but the dog didn't seem to notice. Her heart pounded, and ripples of goose bumps raced over her arms.

The boy called to them. "Hey, you guys, throw down the stick!"

"No!" Hildy yelled back. "Call off your dog or I'm going to whack him."

"Lindy doesn't like boys, except me." The warning was emphasized by the dog's steady, menacing approach. "He must have been hit a lot before I got him, so he sure hates boys—and clubs. Drop yours before he bites you."

Hildy hesitated, uncertain what to do.

Ruby hollered at the boy. "Call off yore dawg and you'n me fight!" she challenged. "If'n I win, you go on and leave us . . ." Her voice trailed off as the dog's behavior suddenly changed.

The dog stopped growling. Slowly, he raised his head. His hackles lay down, and his short tail began to wag.

The stranger swore mightily in surprise. "Well, now. Would you look at that? He likes you! He usually only likes girls, but I never saw him like any boys before, except me."

Hildy and Ruby exchanged glances, then quickly examined their clothing. A slow smile spread over the girls' faces.

Hildy dropped her stick and knelt, holding out the back of her hand so the approaching dog could sniff it.

"Nice doggie," she said.

"He's an Airedale," the stranger informed them as he approached with the sole of his left shoe flapping. "I call him Lindy—after Charles A. Lindbergh. Lucky Lindy. Got myself an aviator's cap just like he wore when he flew *The Spirit of Saint Louis* nonstop from New York to Paris seven years ago. First person to fly across the Atlantic Ocean alone, you know."

Hildy patted the terrier-like dog. "We know about that," Hildy told him defensively.

Lindy turned to wag his tail in greeting to Ruby, and Hildy stood up.

"Howdy," Hildy said, smiling more in relief than in greeting.

"Howdy yourself," the boy replied with a grin. "Name's Spud. Well, that's not my real name, of course. If you knew it and called me by it, I'd bust you in the nose."

"Spud?" Hildy asked, studying the boy.

"For all the spuds I peel to get a meal now and then. I'm hoboing to Chicago."

"All by yourself?" Hildy asked.

The boy bristled and his ruddy face flushed slightly, the color deepening under the freckles. "I'm fourteen!" he snapped.

"Been on my own nearly two years now." There was pride in the words.

Ruby looked up. "Ain't ye a-goin' the wrong way fer Chicago?"

The boy's quick temper flared. "I told you. I'm hoboing. Don't have to go any special direction. Doesn't matter much when I get there, either." He paused, then added, "I didn't catch your names."

Without thinking, Hildy answered, "I'm Hildy." The instant she said it, she realized what she'd done and turned anguished eyes on Ruby.

"Hildy?" Spud repeated. "I thought that was a girl's name?"

"Can be a boy's," Hildy assured him.

"I suppose." Spud seemed doubtful.

"Y'all kin call me Tom," Ruby said quickly.

Spud nodded. "Tom, Hildy, you guys eaten today?"

Before the girls could answer, Spud swung the stick off his shoulder and caught the blue and white polka-dot handkerchief at the end. "I got plenty for all of us. Let's eat while you two tell me about yourselves. I get mighty lonesome for company, hoboing around, you know."

A glance at the sun told Hildy it was around noon, but she didn't want to stop. She wanted to get as far away from Vester and as close to her Uncle Cecil's in Oklahoma as possible. However, Hildy didn't want to tell this young stranger about herself or Ruby. Neither did Hildy want to arouse Spud's suspicions. The sooner they ate with the stranger, the quicker Hildy and Ruby could be on their way again.

Spud spread out the handkerchief on the ground and sat down, thrusting his left foot out. His loose sole flopped down in front of him, and Hildy noticed a large hole in the bottom of the sole. It had been temporarily patched with a piece of cardboard but was already nearly worn through.

Up until now, Hildy hadn't felt an appetite. All her anger, pain, and excitement had hidden that. But at the sight of Spud's food, Hildy was instantly hungry.

"Sliced ham and sweet potatoes," Spud explained, "Help

yourselves. Lady gave them to me this morning when I chopped some wood for her. I already started eating on this biscuit. Had two for breakfast, so I'll finish the last one. But you can have whatever else you want."

"No, thanks . . . Spud," Hildy said. "We've got some corn bread and sweet potatoes of our own." She indicated the tow sacks.

"No, save yours and eat this," the boy insisted. "Meat might spoil in this heat." He broke off a piece of biscuit, handed it to the dog, then ate a bite himself.

The girls took the ham and sweet potatoes and ate in silence, eager to keep their identity hidden and be away from the friendly stranger. But once they started eating, they realized how hungry they were and soon finished all the food they had brought, too.

"Where you guys headed?" Spud asked.

Hildy and Ruby glanced at each other. Hildy shrugged. "No place special."

"You bindle stiffs, too?"

Hildy blinked. "What's that?"

"Hobo, like me. Slang word. Some people use it to mean the stick and handkerchief I carry over my shoulder. Actually, bindle is another slang expression from the Scotch, meaning bedding," he said, sounding like a talking dictionary.

Ruby giggled. "Ye shore talk funny."

Instantly, Spud bristled. His face reddened and he scowled. "Listen. You both have accents. Hildy's isn't so bad, but you, Tom, well, I almost need an interpreter to understand you."

Ruby started to make a cutting reply, but Hildy gripped her arm tightly, and Ruby didn't answer.

Spud rushed on, his face flushed. "I ran away because my old man and I never got along, but I'm going to be somebody someday! Educating myself. I know more words than anybody." He reached into his hip pocket and whipped out a small book, badly battered.

"See this?" he asked. "It's a dictionary. Got all kinds of words in it. Every day I learn a new word."

"Who cares?" Ruby muttered.

Hildy spoke quickly. "Ah, she . . . uh . . . Tom didn't mean anything. Don't take offense."

Spud's face slowly lightened. "None taken," he said, putting the dictionary back in his pocket. "Tell you what, I'll teach both you guys to speak properly if you want."

"We'uns already know how!" Ruby snapped.

"I like new words, Spud," Hildy said quickly. "I'd be glad to learn. But we're going different directions."

The boy shrugged and gave Lindy another bite of biscuit. "I'm in no hurry to get to Chicago. Why don't the three of us hobo together to wherever you're going?"

Hildy started to panic. She and Ruby certainly didn't need anyone complicating their lives, especially this stranger who thought they were boys. Hildy started to protest, but Ruby grabbed her arm.

"Lookee!" Ruby whispered.

Hildy followed her cousin's gaze, then took a short, quick breath. "Vester!" she whispered. "Back there in the trees." Hildy and Ruby jumped up so suddenly that Lindy nearly fell over backward trying to get out of their way.

"Much obliged, Spud," Hildy told him hurriedly, trying to not look at Vester in the distance. He probably hadn't seen them since they weren't moving, she decided. In the woods, anything that moved attracted attention.

"Hey!" Spud exclaimed, looking up at them. "What's going on?"

"No time to explain," Hildy answered shortly. "We've got to get going."

The girls snatched up their tow sacks and hurried into the deep shadows of the heavily wooded area beside the trail. Hildy's heart thumped hard in fear. If Vester caught them now . . .

Ruby was obviously thinking the same thing. The two cousins glanced back to determine whether Vester had seen them.

"Oh no!" Hildy whispered.

Vester was nowhere in sight, but Spud was running after them, his loose sole flopping wildly. He waved. "Wait! Lindy and I are going with you!" he called.

The two girls groaned.

CHAPTER FIVE

HEADING WEST TO TROUBLE

As Spud and Lindy ran toward the girls, Hildy's anger rose. "We can't have him tagging along with us!" she muttered under her breath.

Ruby balled up her fists. "I kin whup him and send him packin'!"

"No," Hildy whispered. "You're too big a girl to go around beating up on boys anymore."

"He don't know I'm a girl."

"And he mustn't find out, either. But he could if you got into a fight. Besides, Vester might see us!"

"Then what're we gonna do?"

"We'll have to let Spud come along for a while, but then we ll slip away from him soon's we can."

"Yeah. The main thing's to git away from Vester."

When the boy and his dog caught up, Hildy took charge. "Spud, you've got to walk faster if you want to keep up with us."

"What's the hurry? Hobos have no time schedule."

"We're not hobos," Hildy explained. "We're going to see relatives in Oklahoma."

"Yeah? Where?"

Hildy hesitated, unwilling to tell too much. "Oh, somewheres in the middle." She increased her pace, anxiously glancing over her shoulder.

Spud walked faster, keeping up with his two companions. "You two running from somebody?"

"Now, why would we be a-doin' that?" Ruby protested.

Spud shrugged. "You're both looking over your shoulders as if you were expecting your fathers to catch up. Well, not mine! He'd never come looking for me. Fact is, he's probably glad I'm gone. One less mouth to feed. Besides, he never cared about me."

There was bitterness in the boy's words mixed with a touch of sadness. Hildy wanted to reach out and touch his arm, to comfort him somehow. She knew how he felt, for sudden painful memories flooded over her.

There was a difference between Spud and herself, however. He had run off, but Molly had left Hildy behind. Spud didn't want to go home, but Hildy desperately wanted to find her family. That wouldn't happen at all if Vester caught up with them first.

Hildy and Ruby set a fast pace, but Spud didn't seem to mind. He always seemed ready for any challenge. He also had an audience to whom he could talk. After a while he asked, "Where you guys from?"

Hildy evaded his question. "Where are you from?"

"I was born in Brooklyn, the youngest of seven brothers and one sister. We're all American-born, although our parents came from Ireland. I don't have either an Irish or a Brooklyn accent, and I'm an Orangeman—you know, a Protestant Irishman."

Hildy didn't know what that really meant and she was reluctant to ask. Spud talked through the afternoon while Hildy and Ruby walked fast, glancing back periodically to make sure Vester wasn't closing in on them.

Spud had developed his love of words through one teacher,

he explained, producing his dictionary again. Miss Krisman had taught the boy to believe that power lay in the proper use of words.

Hildy sighed wistfully. She envied Spud and his dictionary. Unlike Ruby, Hildy loved learning, but she had received all of her education in the same one-room country school with about eighteen other students. Over the years, Hildy had been taught by various relatives of school-board members. But she taught herself a lot, too, through books, until Hildy rightly felt she knew more than some teachers did.

"But," Spud said at length as the three strode along, "I got tired of my old man cussing me and knocking me around, so I took off one day. Found Lindy here about ten months ago, nearly starved. Somebody'd dumped him to die along the road. Guess they couldn't feed him anymore. Fact is, most people can't feed themselves now that this Depression's lasted so long."

Hildy turned to look at Spud. "I keep hearing about the Depression," she remarked, "but I don't really understand it."

Spud looked at her in surprise. "Oh, a depression is 'an economic crisis and period of low business activity,'" he explained.

"That doesn't mean anything to me," Hildy replied. "Everybody's poor in the Ozarks."

Spud cleared his throat. "Well," he began, "a depression isn't money so much as it is people. For example, this depression started with the stock market crash on Wall Street back in '29. In five years, it's become worldwide. But that doesn't tell the human side of it. Everybody's broke. Men are miserable because they've lost their jobs through no fault of their own. And the worst part is that millions of people have lost hope."

Hildy nodded. "Oh, now I understand." She knew about hope. Hope was keeping her going toward Oklahoma with Vester trailing to take her back to Possum Hollow.

Spud turned to Ruby. "How about your father, Tom? He working?"

"Leave my father outta this!" Ruby snapped. She was always

sensitive when anyone asked about her family.

Spud's jaw muscles tightened, and Hildy sensed he didn't like Ruby much. It was also obvious that she didn't care for him, either. Hildy would have to prevent any conflict that might give away the cousins' disguises.

"Tell me more about this depression," Hildy urged.

As they walked on, Spud told of seeing long lines of men standing on sidewalks leading to bread or soup kitchens in big cities. And he explained how the Depression had affected various people he had met in his travels.

The girls kept moving fast, occasionally checking their back trail, while the boy in knickers talked of bankruptcies, bank failures, and the gloom that lay over all of the country.

Spud told of seeing honest, hard-working men "riding the rods," or stealing dangerous rides on freight trains where they could easily be killed. He talked about seeing skilled, educated men sleeping in giant concrete pipes at idle construction sites and men drifting from one place to another, desperately hunting work but finding none.

Hildy nodded soberly. "That's what my daddy did. He went everywhere to find work."

"What has he done?" Spud asked.

"He's picked cotton—so've I—and done about everything. Right now, he's cowboying."

The boy turned to Ruby. "Tom, what's your father do?"

Ruby bristled defensively, but before she could explode with something like "none of your business," Hildy spoke up.

"Ru—Tom doesn't like to talk about his family," Hildy began, picking up a small rock from the trail. "But you know what my daddy used to be?"

Spud shook his head.

"When I was born, my daddy was a sharecropper." She decided there was no harm in telling this strange but friendly boy a little bit about *her* family. But she wouldn't tell him about Molly taking the other kids and running off, leaving Hildy behind like an unwanted dog. She continued. "My daddy once said, 'Hildy, you was born in a sharecropper's cabin, and things sort of went downhill from there. But someday things'll be different.' "

Spud whipped out his dictionary and thumbed through it. Hildy frowned, not understanding his actions.

Spud read aloud. " 'Sharecropper—noun, a tenant farmer who pays a share of the crop as rent.' "

"Means dirt-poor and broke," Hildy said ruefully, throwing the rock into the woods.

Lindy bounded away after the rock, leaping a tumbled-down split-rail fence.

Spud grinned. "You know something, Hildy? You throw just like a girl."

Hildy swallowed hard, realizing that even such a little thing as that was likely to give her and Ruby away. Instantly, Hildy decided they would have to part company with Spud before their secret was discovered. But how could the girls get away?

Lindy trotted back with the rock and dropped it at her feet.

"I can throw all kinds of ways," Hildy said lamely.

Ruby stopped suddenly. "So kin I. You make any more personal cracks 'bout Hildy, and I'll pin yore ears back!"

"Oh, is that so?" Spud bristled, his face flooding red with anger. "You want to settle this right here and now?" He jerked off his aviator's cap and threw it on the ground. Then he raised his arms defensively and curled his big hands into fists.

Hildy quickly stepped between Spud and her cousin as Lindy whined. "Now, stop it, you two!" Hildy gave Ruby a warning look. "We got other problems more important than fighting each other."

"Yeah?" Spud stepped back from the disguised Ruby and lowered his arms. "Like what?"

For a moment Hildy hesitated, unwilling to mention Vester. "Like . . . what're we going to eat for supper?"

"Oh, that's easy!" Spud assured her. "We'll walk right up to somebody's back door and say, 'Have you got any work I can do for a little food?' And the lady will say, 'We're poor as church mice, but I'd never turn a hungry boy away from my door. If you want, you can chop some wood, draw some water from the well, or maybe slop the hogs. Then I'll have a little something for you to eat by the time you're finished.' "

Hildy blinked. "You mean, beg?"

Spud's face flushed in anger. "It's not begging when you exchange work for food." His voice had a sharp edge to it. "That's a fair exchange. Begging's when you implore charity. I never took a thing in my life I didn't work for!"

Ruby bristled at Spud's tone. "There ain't no call to git all het up 'bout it!"

Spud's green eyes snapped with his voice. "Now look here, Tom, I've had about all of your attitude that I can take!"

"Oh, is that so?" Ruby challenged, bringing up her fists. "Ye want to do somethin' 'bout it?"

Hildy stomped her foot. "Stop it, Ruby! Spud! Both of you." Too late, Hildy realized she'd made a slip of the tongue.

"Well, Tom started it," Spud cried angrily, not seeming to notice the slip.

"It doesn't matter!" Hildy exclaimed. "Now, let's just walk along peacefully and try to find a place to work for our supper."

As the trio started walking again over the unfamiliar countryside, their eyes flickered across the ridges and valleys, looking for smoke from a chimney.

Hildy's brow wrinkled in thought as she walked. *I've got to get those two apart before they light into each other*, she thought. *And before Spud finds out we're girls.*

But she didn't know how to separate them. Besides, she found herself sort of wishing Spud could stay with them. Hildy could learn from him. And there was something comforting about having the older boy around. He might be especially welcome if Vester showed up unexpectedly. But sooner or later, if Spud stayed, he and Ruby were sure to tangle.

All of a sudden Spud stopped dead-still. He turned, frowning. "Hildy, a while ago you called Tom 'Ruby.' How come?"

"Hildy did no such a thing!" Ruby protested.

Spud's face started to flush again. "I heard him. Now, why'd he call you that unless your name's not really Tom?"

Before Hildy could think of an answer, she saw smoke rising from a clump of trees. "Look!" she cried, pointing. "A house."

"And there's another one over yonder," Ruby added.

Spud abandoned his question at the possibility of getting something to eat. "Let's try the one on the right," he suggested.

Ruby crossed her arms over her bib overalls in defiance. "I say we try t'other house."

Hildy's mind clicked. She had an idea that would prevent another confrontation. At the same time, it would provide an opportunity to get away from Spud and lessen the chance of Vester finding them. "Why don't we try both?" she suggested. "Spud, how about you going to the house on the right while . . . uh . . . Tom and I go to the other? If either of us gets turned down, we could try the other place."

"What happens if both places give us something?" Spud asked.

"Then we eat and meet back here later." Hildy shot a meaningful glance at Ruby.

She seemed to understand. "Good idee!" Ruby exclaimed. "You take the one on the right, and we'll take this'n. Meet back here later."

As Spud and Lindy took off in one direction and Hildy and Ruby hurried in the other, they had no way of knowing that they were heading for more trouble than they had ever known in their lives.

CHAPTER SIX

RAZORBACKS AND MOONSHINERS

The two girls walked rapidly until they reached the woods. Stopping by a slippery elm, they glanced back. Spud and his dog were out of sight. Instantly Hildy and Ruby broke into a full run, but not toward the smoking chimney they'd seen from the road.

Hildy was panting by the time they leaped a small creek, commonly called a branch. "I sure hate doing this to Spud," she told Ruby.

"I'm right glad to be shed of him."

"We *can* go faster without him," Hildy replied. "We've got to make sure Vester doesn't catch up with us"—She shivered at the thought of their pursuer—"otherwise I'll never find my family."

"We ain't seen no sign of Vester fer quite a spell. Maybe we lost him."

"He'll not give up," Hildy noted sadly. "Well, let's get moving again. I sure hope Molly and the kids are at Uncle Cecil's."

The girls dodged through brush and brambles, avoiding the

house with its cheery wood-smoke fire that promised food. It would be impossible for Spud to follow them and, hopefully, very difficult for Vester. At least the girls' crooked trail would delay pursuit.

In half an hour, they'd taken so many twists and turns in a westerly direction that they found themselves in a densely wooded section of the mountains.

After the girls puffed up another hill, a small, flat area opened before them. A tiny abandoned log church guarded an unkempt cemetery under the trees.

"Let's stop and rest," Hildy suggested.

"I don't like graveyards." Ruby's voice trembled.

"Ruby, you know there're no such things as *haints*."

"I don't know. I've heard so many turrible stories."

"That's all superstitious nonsense, mostly from the old folks. Anyway, I'm not afraid. I've got to stop and catch my breath."

Reluctantly, Ruby sat down by a black haw tree, facing the church, her back to the cemetery. "Well, not fer long," she said.

As Hildy glanced around at the grave markers, her blue eyes were attracted to a small, new mound that had not yet settled. Some wildflowers, still fresh, lay by the simple wooden marker.

She pointed for Ruby's benefit. "That one looks kind of small," she said aloud, still catching her breath. "Like a child's grave." Getting up, she walked over to see the new, hand-painted wooden marker at the head of the grave.

" 'Ezekiel Colter,' " Hildy read, " 'age 14 years, 10 days, killed by a Sawton.' " She straightened up, sadness gripping her insides. "He was awful young."

"What's a Sawton?" Ruby asked.

"Probably a last name."

Ruby jumped up. "Hey! Do ye reckon they's a feud a-goin' on in these here parts, and he was kilt in it?"

"Doesn't seem likely. Feuds happen in other states, I think, but . . ." Leaving the sentence unfinished, she cocked her head and held her breath.

Hildy heard something move in the dense brush at the edge of the unfenced churchyard. "Listen!" Her heart speeded up.

She walked quietly over to stand by Ruby. "Hear it?"

"Shore do. What d'ye reckon it is?"

"Don't know. Animal, maybe. It's low down, close to the ground."

"Let's git outta here!" Ruby turned and rapidly walked away from the church.

Hildy swallowed hard, but the knot of fear that had developed in her throat wouldn't go down. Wordlessly, she turned and followed Ruby, now wishing Spud and his dog were here.

The girls glanced back a few times as they passed the cemetery and the church, then headed for the hardwood forest again with Ruby in the lead.

Suddenly Ruby stopped. Hildy, who was glancing back, bumped into her cousin.

"Shhh!" Ruby warned, staggering slightly from the unexpected blow from behind. She pointed. "Somethin' moved over that-a-way."

Hildy strained to hear and see. Through the thick brush in the dimming late afternoon light, her sharp eyes caught a slight movement where Ruby pointed. "Better try that way," she said softly, jerking her head in the direction of the house they could no longer see. "We can hide behind or in front."

"They'll see us from the house," Ruby whispered. "Let's go back the way we come."

"We might run into Spud!"

"Better him than whoever or whatever's a-hidin' in that brush yonder."

While Hildy hesitated, she heard a short, low grunt from the brush. Instantly, she knew the danger. "Razorbacks!" she whispered fearfully.

Ruby's face registered her own fear of what that meant.

When the girls were little, they had been walking through the woods, picking wildflowers. As they approached a thicket, all at once it exploded with several thin, mean wild hogs. There was no mistaking them for the domestic animals that many people raised around Possum Hollow. Family hogs were wider, heavier, with compact bodies, short tusks and noses that looked as though they had been hammered back.

Razorback hogs were smaller, skinnier, and amazingly fast. They were also meaner and more aggressive. Their long, vicious tusks had been known to rip a person's legs terribly.

"Don't move!" Hildy whispered. "Maybe they'll go away."

"I jist cain't stand here like a stump," Ruby hissed, her voice cracking with fear. "I'm gonna run fer the house."

"You'll never make it," Hildy warned.

It was too late. Ruby exploded from her statue-like position into a wild, panicky run.

Instantly, Hildy heard the warning grunt. Then a big boar popped into view. He pounded furiously after Ruby.

Hildy shrieked. "Look out, Ruby! Behind you!"

The old male razorback stopped stock-still. He swung his ugly snout toward her, his small eyes glaring.

Ruby glanced back but kept running.

The boar was unusually big for a razorback, but he had the characteristic spine that gave him his name. His long nose was covered with dirt where he'd been rooting. Ugly tusks curled upward and outward like glistening swords. His black bristly sides showed old scars from savage fights over the years.

Hildy knew that a hog can run as fast as the average man, so this one could almost surely outrun a half-grown girl. Resisting the urge to bolt, she held still as a stone, hoping to not draw the boar's charge.

He stood, grunting, watching her, ignoring Ruby, who still crashed through the brush off to Hildy's right.

For a moment, Hildy thought everything was going to be all right, that the boar would be content, having scared off any potential threat of danger to himself.

Hildy stole a quick look at Ruby. She was still running hard toward a path in the dense brush ahead of her. Suddenly, with a few startled grunts, a sow with several pigs arose in front of Ruby.

Hildy knew they should have expected that. Hogs are herd animals, even in the wild. She started to shout a warning, but Ruby had already slid to a stop, her arms flailing to keep her balance. Threatened, the sow launched forward, squealing in a blur of fury, heading straight for the defenseless Ruby.

"Oh no!" Hildy moaned. She glanced around for a stick or anything to use as a weapon but saw nothing. Raising her head, she shrieked at the top of her lungs and rushed recklessly toward Ruby and the charging sow.

Startled, the old boar grunted in alarm and swung his narrow snout around. His little eyes glittered. Then he charged Hildy!

"Oh, Lord!" The words escaped her lips in a moaning prayer. Her eyes desperately searched for a place of safety. She didn't see any.

For a second, she hoped Spud would come bursting into the open from the deep shadows of the forest. Maybe Lindy would race in, his short tail raised defiantly, his brown muzzle open and snarling a warning to the girls' attackers.

But that didn't happen.

Instead, something snarled past Hildy's head like an angry hornet. She saw the boar swerve. At almost the same instant, a sharp crack echoed through the woods.

A splintered second later, another rifle shot sounded. Dirt flew in the sow's eyes from the bullet striking the ground in front of her. The mother pig broke off her charge and stopped.

Hildy realized that the second shot had come so soon after the first that it was almost one. That indicated two riflemen.

As the reports drifted away into the distance, Hildy glanced around to see who had fired the shots but saw nothing. She heard only her thundering heart and her ragged breathing as the boar and sow turned away.

Hildy was used to the sound of rifles, but she had never heard bullets pass so close to her. They had come from directly behind her, where she first heard the bushes move.

The mother hog rushed back to her brood, which had scattered and hidden. They erupted in a squealing parade, following her headlong into the brush as the boar smashed his way into another clump of brush.

For a moment, both girls stood frozen in the abrupt silence. Then, realizing they were safe, they heaved a big sigh and slowly turned in the direction of the shots.

But nobody showed. The woods remained still and lifeless. The riflemen seemed to have vanished as completely as the sound of their shots.

Hildy and Ruby eased toward each other through the brush. Their heads twisted this way and that, searching for their rescuers, waiting for them to show themselves. But they didn't.

As the girls reached each other, Hildy had a fearful thought. "Let's get out of here!" Her voice cracked with fear.

"Why? We oughtta thank—"

"No! Let's get away!" Hildy interrupted with a fierce whisper.

"Toward the house?"

"No! Back toward Spud!"

"But . . . what about them—whoever fired those shots?"

"Don't you understand? If they wanted us to see them, they'd have shown themselves." Hildy turned back the way they had come toward the tiny church and the lonely cemetery with its fresh grave.

Ruby hurried to catch up. "Hildy, ye reckon thar really is a feud here'bouts, and whoever done that thar shootin' figured we was their enemies?"

By now Hildy was almost running. "Maybe," she answered. "More likely, it's somebody thinking we're too close to their still."

Ruby nodded, breathing hard. "A still. Of course! Moonshiners. That makes sense."

Hildy and Ruby lived in a "dry" county where liquor manufacture and sale was forbidden by local law. The closest liquor was in Missouri, but even in Arkansas, some rural mountain men like Vester Hardesty violated the law by making and selling their own liquor—moonshine.

Moonshiners had two common characteristics: secrecy and a fierce defense of their stills. It was dangerous to venture close to any still, even by accident.

The back of Hildy's neck began to crawl with fear as she thought of what could happen if she and Ruby had really blundered upon a hidden still. Then she glanced down at her overalls and realized that whoever had fired the shots thought they had saved a couple of boys from razorbacks.

Now, Hildy realized, these same unseen riflemen might be wondering if it would be safe to let the strangers go, wondering if maybe the "boys" would report the location of their illegal operations. Hildy remembered the grave of the fourteen-year-old by the church. Maybe he hadn't died in a feud but had been killed by moonshiners. It didn't matter how it happened; he was dead. The same thing could happen to Hildy and Ruby.

A rifle bolt clicked from the brush, confirming Hildy's fears. Then an idea popped into her head. Reaching up, she snatched off her cap, letting her braids fall down over her shoulders. "Take off your cap, Ruby!" she shouted.

"Why?"

"Because they won't shoot girls!"

Ruby didn't react quickly enough. Hildy's free hand darted out and grabbed her cousin's cap just as a second rifle bolt cocked.

Hildy spun around toward the invisible riflemen in the brush. "We're girls!" she cried, holding her braids straight out from her head, then pointing to Ruby's hair. Both brunette and blond hair were badly mussed from the caps. Hildy raised her voice. "Girls! See?"

Now she was really glad she hadn't let Ruby cut her hair short. It might come in handy sometimes to look like a girl.

There was a long, menacing silence as the girls turned slowly, facing toward the unseen riflemen in the circle of trees. Then very slowly, Hildy started to turn back the way they'd come. "Come on," she urged in a whisper. "Walk slowly, but let's get out of here!"

It was the longest walk Hildy could remember. Every second she expected to hear the crash of a heavy rifle and feel the rip of a homemade bullet. But she kept moving, trying to fight back the sobs of fear that escaped from her tight throat.

It was only when the girls were out of the woods and approaching the dirt road where they'd left Spud that Hildy began to feel hopeful. "I think we made it!" she cried at last.

"Yeah." Ruby's voice sounded strange, as though she was about to cry. "Listen! I hear somebody!"

Both girls stopped, barely breathing.

"Vester?" Hildy whispered.

A popular song drifted through the trees. "Can I sleep in your barn tonight, Mister, for it's cold lying out on the ground. . . ?"

"Spud!" the girls said together.

"Quick!" Hildy cautioned. "Get your cap back on before he sees us."

Hildy had barely finished tucking her braids back under her cap when Spud came swinging briskly out of the woods toward them. Lindy, bounding ahead, saw the girls first and raced forward barking happily, his short tail wagging.

"Hey, you guys okay?" Spud called, waving his hands over his aviator helmet.

"Yes," the girls answered joyfully as one.

"I heard shots." Spud's face showed genuine concern as he got nearer. "What happened?"

Hildy bent to give Lindy a pat as he bounced up to them, his tongue rolling. "Somebody shot at a couple of razorback hogs that were charging us," she explained, surprised at how glad she was to see Spud.

Ruby added, "Shots plumb skeered them hogs off."

"Who fired the shots?" Spud asked as he reached them.

"Moonshiners, maybe," Hildy answered. "They didn't show themselves, just scared off the hogs and then kept out of sight."

Hildy suddenly thought of something. What if Vester was close enough to hear the shots?

Whether he was or not, the incident had cost the girls valuable time. There was no doubt Vester would have closed the gap between them with night falling fast.

And that posed another problem for the girls.

CHAPTER SEVEN

THE SECRET UNCOVERED

S pud," Hildy said, "since you're back, I guess that means they wouldn't give you any work for supper at that house?"

Spud nodded. "Threatened to sic their dogs on me and Lindy. Mountain folk are supposed to be friendly, but I guess they haven't heard about Ozark hospitality in this area."

Ruby sulked. "What're we gonna do now?"

"Keep walking," Spud replied. "See if we can find another house where they're nicer to strangers."

Ruby glanced at the sky. "It's a-gittin' mighty late, an' my stomach feels like it's a-tryin' to eat my backbone. 'Sides that, I don't much like the idee of spendin' a night in the open. Too many wild animals an' mean people 'round."

Hildy felt the same way, but she was driven to escape Vester and find her family. "We'll find something, so don't worry." She forced herself to sound cheerful. "But I think we'd better stay on the road. Safer that way. What do you think, Spud?"

She knew Spud well enough by now to realize that he didn't like authority. He had been on his own for so long that he automatically resisted anyone else's suggestions. By asking his advice, Hildy hoped to head off any antagonism, especially between Ruby and Spud.

The question seemed to ease Spud's independent spirit. "I was just going to suggest the same thing myself."

Hildy took Ruby's arm and deliberately held back a step so Spud could lead the way. The three went on, anxiously searching for another house as the afternoon light rapidly faded.

In a few minutes, they rounded a curve in the deeply rutted, muddy wagon road. Water still gathered in puddles from the last rain.

Hildy was looking down to avoid a puddle when suddenly she noticed something. "Look!" she cried, pointing in front of her. "Wagon tracks."

Spud bent to look more closely. "Fresh, too," he added. "See how the mud's still sliding back into the rut? Can't be too far ahead of us. Come on. If we hurry, maybe we can catch up and get a ride to the driver's house for supper."

As the three ran forward, the sun slid out of sight ahead of them. Deep shadows slipped in quickly, filling the mountains with threats from unseen and unknown dangers.

All of a sudden Lindy, quartering ahead through the mud, barked sharply.

Spud grinned at Hildy and Ruby. "Lindy hears somebody. We'll know who it is in a minute."

As they rounded a curve through the brush that reached well into the road, they heard loud swearing. Hildy cringed a little. She didn't like strong language.

Then they saw a spring wagon loaded with furniture, a brown mule, and an old man. He was as skinny as a fence rail. His overalls and homespun blue shirt hung like those on a scarecrow. He stood in ankle-deep mud, his overalls muddy to the knees. His shapeless hat hung over the brake handle by the high seat.

The wagon's left rear wheel was stuck in mud a quarter of the way to the hubcap. This forced the wagon's right front end up on a strange angle. The long-eared mule stood unconcerned in the traces just beyond the puddle while the man cursed and pulled on the imprisoned wheel.

The driver had looped the reins around his neck and under his left shoulder so both hands were free. But his frail body wasn't strong enough to release the wheel.

Spud appraised the situation from a distance. "His muscles obviously aren't very strong, but he's sure got powerful lungs," he commented. "I haven't heard anyone cuss that much since the last time my old man got mad at me. What d'you say we give the old curmudgeon a hand?"

Hildy didn't know the meaning of the big word Spud had just used, but she understood generally what he meant. *Curmudgeon*, she repeated the word to herself, rolling the word around in her mind as she and the others hurried toward the old man.

Hildy decided right then that she was definitely going to learn how to speak as Spud did. She had always done well in the one-room school, but everyone spoke the same and used the same words, so she'd never thought about using new ones. Yet in those moments as they approached the swearing, perspiring man in the road, Hildy's decision was made.

Spud reached the man first. "Give you a hand, Mister?" he offered.

The old man had been so angry and was concentrating so hard on his problem that he hadn't heard the dog bark or seen the youngsters approaching. "I'd be much obliged, boys," he replied, wiping his perspiring brow with the back of a mud-splattered hand. "This hyar mule hain't worth a Continental when it comes to pullin' outta a mudhole."

Hildy's natural inclination was to take charge, but not wanting to upset Spud, she asked him what he thought they should do.

Spud seemed to swell a little with importance. He glanced at the wagon and then around at the thick brush beside the road. "Let's drag some brush out here and put it under the stuck wheel," he suggested. "Then we can find a long, stout pole to place under the back end of the wagon. We can pry on that while this gentleman commands the mule to pull. With the brush making a solid place for the wheel, I think the wagon'll come right out."

The frail man nodded thoughtfully. "We oughtta lighten the load fu'st, though," he said.

Wordlessly, the youngsters began unloading the wagon of its homemade furniture. Except for her father, Hildy didn't know anyone who had moved from one house to another. People in the hills tended to find a place, settle down, and stay.

When the furniture rested on the high ground beside the road, they followed Spud's earlier suggestions. With the wagon lighter, the brush and stout green pole in place, the old man took the reins and stood beside the left front wheel.

He clucked to the mule. "Huyah! Brownie, giddyap!"

With a creaking of leather and rattling of chains, the mule took a step forward. The singletree straightened behind him as he took out the slack. Then he leaned into the padded collar, and the wagon began to move.

"It's coming!" Spud grunted, pushing up hard on the green pole beside Hildy and Ruby. "All together now."

A few seconds later, the stuck wagon wheel came free and rolled onto solid ground.

With glad cries, the three youngsters brushed the mud off their hands and approached the old man.

"Whoa! Whoa, now, Brownie!" he called. As the mule slacked off, the man reached up, took his hat off the brake handle and smiled through crooked, yellow teeth. "Much obliged, boys!" He studied them thoughtfully. "Don't rec'lect seein' y'all here'bouts."

Hildy's heart beat faster, but Spud swelled with pride. "We're hoboing," he explained.

Hildy cringed inwardly at the word.

The old man's pale blue eyes peered out from under wide gray eyebrows. "Runnin' away, are ye?" He shrugged. "Well, ye done me a kindness, so I don't rightly keer 'bout sech things. Git in. We'll be late a-gittin' in to the house, but my mizzus will be plumb tickled to have company. Yore more'n welcome to a bite to eat an' a place to sleep."

Hildy sighed with relief, happy to get a jump on Vester by hitching a ride.

After reloading the furniture, the three youngsters sat on the back of the wagon and dangled their feet above the muddy road as the little man drove off. Spud tried to get Lindy to ride up with them, but the dog preferred to trot behind the wagon.

The driver was obviously glad for company. Raising his voice and talking over his shoulder so his passengers could hear him, he introduced himself as Ezra Highton. He explained that his older brother had died a widower, leaving his few belongings to Ezra. "So I done gone over and loaded his stuff onta the wagon, though I hain't got the foggiest notion where t' put the stuff. The mizzus and me got us a tiny house, and it's already full from a lifetime of livin'."

"How far is your house?" Hildy asked.

"Not much farther, mebby an hour," the old man replied. Clucking encouragement to the mule, he slapped the reins gently on the animal's flanks.

The man's voice droned on for a while; then finally it slowed and stopped.

On Hildy's left, Spud rested against a goose-down pillow, his hands laced behind his head. At first, Hildy thought he was gazing at the sky. Then she heard him snoring lightly.

Hildy glanced to her right, where Ruby stared moodily into the darkness behind the wagon. "What're you thinking about?" Hildy asked softly.

"I was jist a-wishin' I knew fer sure if'n my pa was alive or daid."

Hildy sighed. "I wish you did, too."

"I'd ruther be a orphan fer sure than what people say I am. Either way, it's not my fault!"

Hildy tried to sound hopeful. "Maybe your father really is alive and you'll find him someday."

"Oh, shore," Ruby responded bitterly. "How'd I ever do that, huh?" She leaned back against a straw-filled mattress and said no more, eventually dozing off.

A full moon came up behind the wagon as it continued west,

and moonbeams filtered through the trees on the heavily for-
ested ridges. There were shadows, but Hildy no longer felt such
intense danger, not even from Vester. He was probably miles
behind by now.

But Hildy had mixed feelings about her other problems. The
first shock of being abandoned by her stepmother had worn off,
but self-doubt and guilt soon replaced it. *Maybe if I'd tried harder
or helped more with the kids, Molly wouldn't have left me behind*, she
thought.

Hildy's thoughts flipped to Granny. Her stomach twisted in
pain at remembering what the old woman had done. Hildy
wasn't quite sure she hated her grandmother, but the girl's emotions were so intense that hatred wasn't far off the mark.

"Mama wouldn't have liked that," Hildy told herself sadly.
Hildy's mother had been a God-fearing woman who taught love
and tolerance. Hildy had considered herself a Christian since
she was a little girl, but that had changed when her mother died.
Shaken in her faith, she hadn't prayed in a long time. She didn't
like to admit it, but she was mad at the Lord.

Hildy forced herself to think about the immediate future.
How could she and Ruby keep their secret from Spud and Mr.
and Mrs. Highton when everyone prepared for bed? Mountain
houses were small, and it was logical for the host family to place
the three "boys" in the same room. Hildy worried about how to
keep that from happening.

I'll just have to work that out when the time comes, she told herself. *But we can't let Spud or the others know we're girls. And by and
by, we've got to leave Spud behind*.

The full moon filled the night with an unforgettable pale,
pleasant light. Barely above the mountaintops, it seemed to be
rolling along, keeping pace with the wagon, like a giant silver
dollar. But it was now on the left, or east, and no longer behind.
That meant the wagon had turned south.

Hildy twisted around, disturbing Ruby slightly. Hildy raised
her voice. "Mr. Highton, why'd you change directions?"

The driver turned so the moonlight fell on his leathery,
weathered face. "We done turned off the main road onto the

one that leads to my place. Be thar direc'ly," he replied. "Gid-dyap, mule! Reckon these boys are as hongry as me."

Hildy started to reach over to awaken Ruby and Spud, but changed her mind. Her thoughts leaped ahead. *What if Molly and the kids aren't at her brother's when we get there? What if Uncle Cecil won't tell me where they are? What if I can't find them? What if . . . ?*

Hildy shook her head to stop the terrible thoughts. *I'll find them!* she told herself fiercely. *I'll do it, somehow!*

Her thoughts were abruptly interrupted when Lindy barked sharply, jarring Spud and Ruby from their naps. They sat up just as a hound bayed out of the night ahead of the wagon.

The old man raised his voice. "That's ol' Blue a-tellin' my mizzus that I'm a-comin'. Reckon she'll be mighty surprised to see what else I brung 'sides this furniture."

Hildy turned, expecting to see a coal oil lamp in a window. In a moment, through the trees, she saw the pale orangish glow that showed the way home for a weary family traveler. Hildy wished that light were for her, that her family were waiting anxiously for her as Mrs. Highton was waiting for her husband.

When they arrived, Mrs. Highton, a large woman—the exact opposite of her husband—met them at the door and welcomed the three youngsters warmly. "Come in, boys," she said. "Cain't rec'lect the last time chillern was in this house."

Hildy surveyed the inside of the house with dismay. It was a single large room with a lean-to kitchen and stairs leading up to a sleeping loft. A large double bed stood in one corner of the main room, and Hildy guessed it had been put there when the couple got too old to climb the stairs.

Mrs. Highton chided her husband for being so late and scaring her half to death. But when Ezra explained what had happened, Mrs. Highton's tone softened.

Her husband spoke to her mildly. "Now if yore a-goin' to jaw at me, reckon me'n the boys'll take the lantern an' go un-harness the mule so's we kin have some peace and quiet."

"Jist take one of the boys," Mrs. Highton suggested. "Ain't but one mule to unharness, and I got to set five plates. The other two boys kin he'p me."

Spud's face showed disgust at the prospect of doing "woman's work." "I'll help you, Mr. Highton," he offered. "Tom and Hildy'll be glad to set the table, won't you, boys?"

Hildy and Ruby nodded, although Ruby seemed irritated with Spud's high-handed attitude.

Spud and the old man walked outside.

While Hildy and Ruby helped prepare the table, Hildy noticed Mrs. Highton studying the girls out of the corner of her eyes.

In half an hour, everyone sat down to a late supper of fried squirrel, which Mrs. Highton had kept warm on the small kitchen range. Spud removed his aviator's helmet, but both Hildy and Ruby kept their caps on.

Ruby quickly explained. "We ketch head colds real easy-like, so we got to keep 'em on."

Hildy saw Mrs. Highton's eyes narrow suspiciously. As everyone started eating, the old woman leaned over Hildy's shoulder and whispered in her ear. "You and Tom is girls, ain't ye?"

CHAPTER
EIGHT

UNEXPECTED HOPE

Hildy's stomach began to knot as she glanced at Mrs. Highton. The woman, with a look of triumph, got up from the table and headed for the kitchen.

Now what? Hildy wondered. If Mrs. Highton were anything like ol' Miz Nayton, her neighbor back home, soon everyone would know that Hildy and Ruby weren't boys. And if by chance Vester came this way and talked to the Hightons, he would learn his quarry was in disguise.

Hildy carefully lifted her right foot under the table and lightly touched Ruby's leg. When her cousin looked up, Hildy mouthed the words, *She knows!*

For a moment, Ruby frowned, then followed Hildy's gaze toward the kitchen. Ruby's eyes opened wide in understanding.

Hildy scooted her chair back from the table. "I'm finished. Uh . . . Tom, if you are too, let's go help Mrs. Highton. Mr. Highton and Spud, you just go on enjoying yourselves."

The menfolk barely nodded as they continued their conversation.

As Hildy and Ruby started toward the tiny lean-to kitchen, Ruby whispered, "She knows?"

Hildy nodded. "We've got to tell her the whole story so she won't tell her husband and Spud—especially Spud! We've got to try convincing her to keep our secret."

"Ye mean . . . tell her ever'thin'?"

"Everything."

As the girls entered the kitchen, Mrs. Highton turned from where she was heating a kettle of water on the stove. Her eyes reflected both triumph and confusion.

"Mrs. Highton," Hildy began in a low voice. "You're right about us, but if we tell you why, will you keep it to yourself? Don't tell your husband or Spud?"

"Spud don't know?"

Ruby shook her head. "No, he don't. We jist met him today."

The old woman studied the girls with probing blue eyes. "Y'all tell me the bonded truth?"

Hildy and Ruby nodded.

"Let's step outside so's we kin talk," Mrs. Highton said quietly.

As they walked out to the cistern and sat down on the curbing, Lindy and Blue ran up to them.

"Shoo, Blue!" Mrs. Highton hissed. "Git!"

Lindy wagged his stub tail and Mrs. Highton changed her tone. "Reckon this'n kin stay."

Absently, Hildy patted Spud's dog while she talked. Slowly, reluctantly, she told about coming home to find her stepmother had moved, taking Hildy's sisters and one brother with her. Hildy's voice began to break as she recounted how her grandmother had betrayed her and how Vester Hardesty was on their trail.

Then Ruby briefly explained that she was an orphan and cousin to Hildy and that they had to find Hildy's family before Vester caught up with them.

"So," Hildy added, "you see why it's important that nobody knows we're girls. We've got to get to my Uncle Cecil's place near Blue River in Oklahoma as soon as possible."

Mrs. Highton listened in silence, but when they had finished, the old woman cleared her throat. "I don't hold with runnin' off like ye done, Hildy," she began slowly, "but I reckon a young gal's place is with her family. As fer Ruby, I kin unnerstan' ye a-goin' with Hildy. Nothin' behind to keep ye, I reckon."

"Then you won't tell on us?" Hildy asked breathlessly.

"Nary a word, not even to my husbun'. And if that thar Vester comes a-lookin' here, he won't git nothin' outta me but the time of day. Maybe not even that."

Hildy reached out and impulsively gave Mrs. Highton a hug. "Thank you," she whispered.

The old woman brushed aside the demonstration of thanks and affection. She frowned. "Blue River, ye said? That's rollin' prairie country."

Hildy shrugged. "I've never been there."

Mrs. Highton leaned forward. "Our boy, Seth, cowboyed thar when he come home from France after the war," she explained. "Then he moved back here. But he tol' me all about that southwestern part of Oklahoma. Had him a sweetheart thar, but she up and married somebody else oncet when he was t'home here. Like to killed him when he heerd the news. Never married, he didn't. Still lives alone back in these here hills."

Hildy heard sadness in the old woman's voice and instinctively reached out, lightly touching the woman's arm. "I'm sorry," she murmured.

Mrs. Highton's eyes were shiny with unshed tears when she looked up at the girls. "All Ezra's and my other chillern died— all three of 'em. Fevers took 'em, mostly. I was jist 'bout to give up on ever bein' a grandma when our boy come in last week with some news."

The old woman paused, then added, "Seth done learned that his old sweetie is a widder woman. Some kind of a accident 'bout a year ago to her husbun'. So Seth's a-goin' to call on her. And maybe—jist maybe they'll git hitched, and I'll have me a gran'baby someday."

"You mean your son's going to Oklahoma?" Hildy felt her heart speed up at this faint glimmer of hope.

"Yep. Right near Blue River."

"When?" The word almost exploded from Hildy's mouth.

"Tomorry!"

"Tomorrow?"

"Bright and early. Say, I jist had me a thought! I'm a-thinkin' he might have room fer a couple passengers in that thar Model T he done bought fer the trip!"

Hildy and Ruby exchanged hopeful glances, then grinned.

The old woman reached out and patted each of them on the shoulder. "Let me study some on proper sleeping arrangements fer tonight, and you gals git some rest. Come daylight, I'll take ye acrost the hill yonder where Seth lives and see if he'll take ye with 'im."

Hildy nearly floated through the rest of the evening. She didn't hear much of the conversation between Spud and the old man, but Mrs. Highton seemed to take special delight in helping the disguised girls. At bedtime, she put Hildy and Ruby in the loft bed and had Spud sleep on an old army cot in the lean-to kitchen.

As thoughts and questions buzzed around in her head, Hildy lay awake a long time. She didn't mean to pray, but as she looked up at the darkened rafters and thought about how kind Mrs. Highton was and the possibility of getting to Oklahoma with Seth, she whispered, "Thanks, Lord."

She tried to sleep, but couldn't. Doubts began nibbling on her mind.

Ruby apparently had the same fears. "What'll we do if'n her son won't take us?" she whispered.

Hildy thought for a moment before answering softly, "Then we'll find another way."

"What 'bout Spud?"

Hildy had considered that question with mixed feelings. She would have liked to have the boy along, but sooner or later, he and Ruby would get into an argument that Hildy couldn't stop. And, eventually, he would be sure to discover their secret. "You and I have to get to Uncle Cecil's, but Spud doesn't," she replied firmly.

"He'll be pow'rful mad."

Hildy sighed softly into the darkness. "I suppose he will, but we'll never see him again, so it won't matter."

"I guess yore right, Hildy."

The girls lapsed into silence, and Hildy thought about Spud. Guilt rose around her and made her uncomfortable. He deserved better than to be left behind without a word. But Hildy's overpowering drive to find her stepmother and the kids before it was too late made everything else take second place.

Hildy didn't think she would sleep at all, but she jumped when something lightly tapped at the edge of the loft. It took her a moment to realize that the tap came from a broom handle in Mrs. Highton's hands. Hildy peered over the top of the stairs.

The old woman laid her finger across her lips in warning. Hildy nodded and turned back to awaken Ruby.

Quietly, being careful not to disturb Mr. Highton or Spud, the girls dressed and gathered their belongings into their tow sacks. Carrying their shoes, they tiptoed down the stairs from the loft and out the front door.

I feel terrible, sneaking out on Spud like this, Hildy thought, *but I've got no choice!*

The barest hint of dawn touched the tops of the hills and trees along the ridge. The dogs ran up to them with wagging tails, but Mrs. Highton warned them in whispers to be quiet.

As the girls sat on the cistern curbing and slipped their shoes on, Lindy thrust his muzzle into Hildy's hands. Impulsively, she gently ruffled Lindy's ears. "You take good care of Spud," she whispered. Giving the Airedale a final pat, she stood up. "Stay," she commanded softly. "Stay."

Then she turned and silently followed the old woman and Ruby across the lot, beyond the woodpile, through a tumbling down gate in the split-rail fence, and into the silent woods.

Once Hildy looked back. The log house stood silent in the first light of day. *Spud*, she thought, *please try to understand*. She didn't look back again.

A little later, Mrs. Highton and the two girls topped the final rise. As Hildy looked down into a clearing, she saw a tiny house and a lone man in overalls leaning into the front seat of a Model T Ford. He had removed the cushion and was dipping a stick into something.

When Mrs. Highton called to him, he stopped, looked up, and turned around, still holding the stick.

Hildy saw at once that Seth Highton was about the age of her father. Tall and rawboned, he had immense, work-hardened hands and a square jaw that jutted defiantly from his powerful neck.

He listened to his mother's explanation of why she had brought the girls along the trail. Hildy held her breath while Mrs. Highton talked. Slowly Hildy relaxed as the old woman kept the girls' identity secret.

"So, Seth," the woman concluded, "I was a-wonderin' if'n y'all had room fer Hildy and Tom to ride along to Oklahoma?"

The tall, lanky young man considered the two overall-clad visitors for a moment, then nodded. "Reckon I kin squeeze ye in somm'ers." He jerked his chin toward the black sedan.

"Thank you kindly, Mr. Highton!" Hildy exclaimed. "We'll work or do anything we can to pay you back."

"Sounds fair, but call me Seth. I 'spect my ma done tol' ye why I'm a-goin'?" He didn't wait for an answer. "I'm travelin' light 'cause I'm not shore what kinda welcome I'll git after all these years. Well, I was jist 'bout to leave. Checked the gasoline." He indicated the stick, which glistened wet in the sunlight. "I'll git the cap back on the tank, and then ye two boys kin put the seat cushion in place and we're on our way."

Hildy and Ruby grinned with happy anticipation as they worked the stiff seat into place. Yet Hildy was eager to be moving, anxious to keep ahead of Vester. Sooner or later, he would follow the girls' trail to the Hightons'. But by then, in the car, the girls should be far away.

Seth shoved an old cardboard suitcase from the backseat onto the floorboard.

"Boys, throw yore tow sacks thar by my stuff and git in whilst I crank 'er up. Then we're on our way." Seth turned to his mother, hugged her briefly, and grinned at his passengers.

"Ma and me done said goodbye afore sundown last night. So I reckon we'uns don't have to do it long this mornin'."

The girls stood gazing at the first automobile they had ever

seen up close. It was a post-war model, black, with high fenders
and no sides above the doors. Seth walked to the driver's side
and reached in. A buzzing sound made Hildy jump back.

Seth chuckled. "Ain't nothin' to be afeered of. It's jist what
they call the ignition. Now, I'll jist turn the crank up front here,
and if she don't backfire and break my arm, well, we're ready
to roll."

Hildy and Ruby watched, wide-eyed, as he walked around
to the front of the Model T, bent over, and gripped the crank
that hung in the exact middle of the car. Then he gave the crank
a couple of turns. The engine started so suddenly that both
Hildy and Ruby leaped back.

Seth reached over to the left of the radiator and pulled a little
wire circle barely sticking out from beside the motor. "Gotta
choke 'er a mite," he explained, "—give 'er a mite more gas."

The motor began running faster until the whole car quivered.
It vibrated so hard it inched forward.

Seth ran around and slid under the wheel. "Creeps like that
ever' time I start 'er, no matter how hard I set the hand brake,"
he explained above the noise. "Well, ye two better jump in afore
this here Tin Lizzie goes off to Oklahoma all by herself."

There was no back door, only an outline of one. Hildy and
Ruby stepped up on the high running board, ducked their heads
to miss the black top that could be folded down, and threw their
legs over the side. In a moment, they were sitting excitedly on
the black horsehair-filled backseat.

Hildy looked out at Mrs. Highton, who was waving at them.
"Goodbye!" Hildy called. "Thanks for everything!"

"Yeah!" Ruby echoed. "Thanks!"

Seth leaned out over his small door in front. "So long, Ma,"
he said. "I hope I come back with Rachel to git hitched over at
ol' Bethel."

"Me, too!" his mother called. "Bye, y'all!"

Suddenly the car leaped ahead. The girls, who had never
ridden in anything faster than a wagon pulled by a team of
horses, fell backward in the seat. Then they grinned at each
other.

"We're on our way!" Hildy cried. "Let's just hope that Molly and the kids are still there when we arrive."

But Hildy had an uneasy feeling that she was already too late.

CHAPTER
NINE
—

PERILS OF THE ROAD

The excitement of their first automobile ride kept Hildy's and Ruby's heads swinging from side to side as they slowly bounced along dirt and then gravel roads. The gravel slipped under the wheels and made the car bounce terribly.

Seth Highton treated his passengers like any boys their age. He apparently assumed they would be interested in anything mechanical, like the aging Model T Ford. The girls sat there in their overalls and boys' caps and listened politely, but they didn't really care how the car worked except for two incidents.

The first came when a loose domestic pig suddenly dashed into the rutted roadway. To stop the car in time, Seth not only grabbed the hand brake and pulled back hard, but he also jammed his foot down on a floorboard pedal. The Ford slid to a shuddering stop, and the pig disappeared into the roadside underbrush.

As the girls relaxed after the abrupt scare, the rawboned mountaineer gave an explanation. "Slammed 'er inta reverse." He pointed to the three pedals on the floorboard. "Clutch, brake, and reverse. Reg'lar brakes ain't all that good, so kickin' 'er inta reverse helps stop . . . sometimes."

The girls realized the Model T's uniqueness when they compared its braking system with a wagon's brakes that brought a visible shoe into contact with the wheel when a handle was operated.

In an hour or so, Seth started up a hill steeper than any encountered so far. That's when the girls experienced another fascinating aspect of the car.

Nearing the top of the hill, the engine sputtered, coughed and died. Seth swiveled in the seat, stuck his head out the window, and let the silent vehicle start rolling back downhill.

Hildy leaned forward, placing her hands anxiously on the back of the front seat. "What's the matter?"

"Nothin' much," the driver answered. "It's jist that the thing called a carburetor hain't gittin no more gas. The fuel comes from what they call gravity flow. Like water, gasoline cain't run uphill. So, tryin' to climb this here extra steep hill keeps the gas from a-gittin' whar it belongs to make the engine keep a-runnin'."

Ruby stuck her head over the front seat. "What're ye a-doin'?"

"Backin' down to the bottom," Seth explained.

Sudden panic seized Hildy. "You mean we're going back to your place?" she exclaimed.

The tall, lanky young man smiled tolerantly. "No, we're jist gonna let her roll back down to the bottom of this here hill whar she'll be on the level."

"Then what?" Hildy asked, still panicking. She could just see her chances of finding her family in Oklahoma slipping away because of something called a gravity flow carburetor.

Seth shrugged. "Then we'll turn 'er 'round and back up this hill." When the car reached level ground, Seth got out, cranked the engine, crawled back under the wheel, and turned the car around.

"Here we go," he said, again leaning out the driver's side and looking behind him.

Hildy heard the engine speed up. The car began to move in reverse, shuddering and shaking, bouncing up the ruts in the steep hill.

As the Model T continued to chug steadily up toward the top of the hill, Seth explained what was happening. "With the engine downhill, the gasoline flows from the tank under the front seat to the carburetor, so it works jist fine."

When he reached the top of the hill, he found a place wide enough to again turn around, then continued on toward Oklahoma.

The gravel roads looked fairly smooth, but they were really terribly rough and filled with potholes. The Model T pitched, shuddered, and sometimes seemed to stagger. Hildy began to feel a little sick to her stomach, but she had never heard of motion sickness. She thought she was feeling ill from the fried squirrel she had eaten the night before.

Hildy wondered if she should say anything to Ruby. A quick glance showed that Ruby was also feeling nausea. She was perspiring slightly and opening and closing her mouth like a fish.

Hildy whispered, "You sick to your stomach?"

"A little," Ruby admitted. "Musta been somethin' I et."

Seth overheard and turned to look at his passengers in the backseat. "Car sickness, most likely," he said. "Sometimes it he'ps to ride in the front seat. One of ye can ride up here with me a while, then trade off."

He stopped right in the middle of the road, but it didn't matter. They had seen only one horse and buggy and two wagons since they had hit the main road.

Hildy looked at Ruby again. She looked more miserable than Hildy felt. "Uh . . . Tom . . . why don't you climb up front first?" she suggested.

Ruby nodded wordlessly and obeyed.

Seth drove on. "Sometimes it he'ps if'n ye stick yore haid outta the winder so's to catch the breeze," he recommended. "I'll open the windshield so fresh air'll blow direc'ly on both of ye." He paused. "And don't look 'round close," he cautioned. "Look away out inta the distance. That'll he'p, too."

Hildy watched as the driver released a screw and pushed on the glass. The windshield divided, swinging away so that half of the glass was inside the car and the other extended over the hood. The resulting breeze seemed to help Ruby, and she scrunched down and relaxed.

Hildy tried sticking her head out over the side, but that was too uncomfortable. Finally she gave up and settled down against the back cushion, keeping her eyes on the horizon.

Soon she felt better, and as Ruby began a conversation with Seth, Hildy only half listened, her mind drifting.

Seth talked about the Dust Bowl that extended over areas of the prairie states. The topsoil had been blown away in great wind storms, he said, because the farmers had plowed too much, burned the grass, or let their cattle overgraze the natural grass cover.

"Parts of Oklahoma've been turrible hard hit by the dust storms," he told Ruby. "People are a-givin' up the land, loadin' mattresses on the roof of their old wrecks of cars, and headin' fer Californy."

California! The word made Hildy's heart leap with hope. Her father had a job there. If Hildy could find her stepmother and the kids at Molly's brother's place—Uncle Cecil's—then the family could be reunited. Someday Hildy's father would come get them, and the whole family would move to California. That's where Hildy expected to find what she had promised her sisters: their "forever home."

The words echoed in Hildy's heart like a happy song. A home where they would never have to move again. No more sharecroppers' cabins. No more tumbled-down shacks in the Ozarks. Instead, they would own a house that was really a *forever* home.

Maybe it would even have running water indoors, instead of having a well and cistern outside. There could be a pump in the kitchen, so there would be water for dishes just by pumping on a metal handle. Why, there might even be one of those things she had heard about called a bathroom. That way, nobody would have to run through the rain or snow to the little house out in back because there wouldn't be any such place.

Hildy wondered if there might even be electric lights in this California home. Hildy had heard that electricity worked off a switch, and the lights were much brighter than coal-oil lamps. But then, those things really didn't matter, Hildy decided. What did matter was that all her family would be together forever.

Before that could happen, however, Hildy had to find her stepmother and square things away with her. There obviously had been a terrible misunderstanding. Otherwise, Molly wouldn't have believed Granny and slipped away without saying a word to Hildy.

She again dealt with guilt feelings. *I'll tell Molly it was really my fault. If I had tried to be closer to her and been better with the kids, she wouldn't have left me behind.*

On the other hand, she argued with herself, *it's not all my fault, either. Part of it is Molly's. She should have asked me if I wanted to stay with Granny. Molly should have known I'd never give up the kids and Daddy for anybody, not even Granny.*

Hildy frowned, trying to decide how she felt about Granny. *I thought all grandmothers were supposed to be nice and wonderful*, she told herself with sadness. *But I guess some can do awful things like Granny did, saying she loved me and that's why she did it. But that's not love; that's being selfish.*

I do love her, the girl decided, *in spite of the terrible thing she did. And when I work things out with Molly, I'll write Granny.*

The gentle drone of Ruby and Seth's conversation from the front seat lulled Hildy into a half-sleep.

A sudden loud bang jerked Hildy upright in the seat. Her eyes popped open. "What happened?" she cried.

Seth steered the Model T onto the shoulder and stopped. "Sounded like a pun'ture. A tahr blew out." He got out of the Ford and walked around the front.

The girls followed and stood with the driver by the right front wheel, gazing at the tire flat against the gravel road.

Seth sighed. "Reckon I'll have to patch the tube. You boys stretch yore legs if'n ye want while I change the tahr."

The disguised girls offered to help, but Seth shook his head.

While they waited, Hildy and Ruby started walking aimlessly along the deserted country road.

"He's nice," Ruby whispered. "I wish I had me a daddy like

him." She glanced back at Seth and added softly, "I jist wish I had me a daddy."

Hildy thought they were about the saddest words she'd ever heard. "Maybe you'll find him someday," Hildy said with a conviction she did not feel.

Ruby took a deep breath and slowly let it out. "The truth," she mused. "That's all I'd like to know. Well, that ain't egzackly right, neither. I'd shore admire to find him—if'n he's alive."

When the girls returned to Seth, he had finished patching the inner tube and placed it inside the tire carcass. He let his passengers help pump up the tire and put the tools away.

"As long as we're stopped, we may's well eat," Seth reasoned. "I got enough for all of us. I heerd a branch runnin' back off'n the road a piece. We kin wash up thar."

After lunch, Hildy rode in the front seat, and Ruby tried to stretch out in the back.

Hildy thought Seth might have talked himself out with Ruby, but he hadn't. Holding both of his big hands on the steering wheel, he remarked, "Tom done tol' me all about hisself; now, what 'bout you?"

Hildy shrugged, feeling sudden anxiety over what Ruby had said. One thing was certain, however. Ruby had not disclosed that the two passengers were girls dressed up in overalls and boys' caps.

"There's not much to tell," Hildy replied. "I'm just trying to find my stepmother and patch up a misunderstanding."

"Reckon she'll still be at her brother's ranch?"

"I hope so. And the ranch isn't his. He works for someone."

"Doin' what?"

"I don't know."

"Maybe pasture riding. I've done that. Rode dusk to dawn ever' day. Ketch a new hoss ever' mornin'. Lonely work."

"Cecil's not my real uncle. My mother died and Dad married Molly. Cecil's Molly's brother."

Hildy paused, her old fears returning. Every mile was taking her farther from Vester's threat, yet every mile also brought her closer to where her family should be. What if Molly had gone on, taking the kids with her? Would Hildy ever be able to catch up with them? And when she did, would Molly take Hildy back into the family or turn her away?

Hildy swallowed hard, thinking, *I guess we'll soon find out.*

CHAPTER
TEN

UNCLE CECIL'S NEWS

As the hours ground on, the Ozarks fell behind, and the Ford chugged along well into Oklahoma. Darkness settled but Seth did not stop. He simply turned on the weak headlights, and they bounced and jiggled on an empty, unwinding stretch of sandy road. The closer Seth got to his destination, the harder he pushed the rattling old Model T.

Hildy didn't mind. She understood the driver's anxiety to find out if his one-time sweetheart would welcome him or reject him. That was fine with Hildy. The sooner she reached Uncle Cecil's place, the sooner she'd know about Molly and the kids. Maybe they would be there.

Hildy turned around to look at Ruby. She was curled up asleep in the backseat, unmindful of the jostling ride. Hildy was glad her cousin could rest.

She stared ahead again as the headlights barely poked a white tunnel in the darkness. Hildy could occasionally see small wild animals, mostly rabbits, in the beams. Some of the rabbits hopped alongside the slow-moving car. Others simply sat in the road, forcing the driver to swerve to miss them.

Seth growled. "Either they ain't never seen many cars, or

else they're a-tryin' to commit suicide. I cain't rightly say's how I blame them much. Reckon if'n they could, they'd do like ever'body else and move to Californy."

He turned to look at Hildy. "People think that thar is the Promised Land, like the Good Book says," he continued. "But that hain't so no more. I hear tell that they's so many thousands of them a-comin' that the people already out there are meetin' the new ones at the Californy border. They've used pick handles and such, tryin' to turn 'em back by force."

Hildy's stomach gave a sickening lurch. Would that happen to them when she finally caught up with her family and they went to California?

No, she told herself, *because Daddy's already out there working someplace. Wish I knew where. Well, Uncle Cecil might know, and I'll soon see him.*

For a moment, Hildy thought about Vester, then shook her head. *We've lost him for sure.* Yet somehow she didn't quite believe that.

Seth swerved to avoid another rabbit. "I hear tell they's one piece of paved road in all the West," he said. "That's near Salt Lake City in Utah. They got a few miles of concrete road. But we're plumb lucky to have this here sand. Shore beats them dirt roads we had before."

Hildy wasn't worried about concrete roads. She was hungry. But Seth drove nonstop until scattered lights in the distance marked a small town. Although the girl had never seen electric lights, she recognized them at once. They were marvelous to see! The houses that were well-lit had power. The homes with a weak yellow glow still had the familiar coal-oil lamps.

At the edge of town, Seth finally stopped for gas. With a squeal of brakes, the Ford came to a shuddering stop. Ruby woke up, and the girls looked around at the new surroundings. Bare light bulbs hung on long cords in the combination store-cafe. One glass-topped gasoline pump stood outside.

"Boys," Seth announced, "here's thu'ty cents." He handed a nickel and a quarter to Hildy. "Go inside an' order six hamburgers. Then ye better go out back whilst they're a fryin' them burgers. I'll pump the gas and we'll be on our way agin."

Hildy and Ruby dashed into the roughly made frame building that served as a restaurant and store. After ordering the burgers, they eagerly ran for the little house out back, leaving Seth alone.

While Ruby used the one-holer, Hildy stood outside and watched Seth work a handle on the side of the gasoline pump. The fuel sloshed into a clear glass container marked off by gallons. When the container was nearly full, Seth removed the Model T's front seat cushion, took off the tank's big cap, inserted the hose nozzle, and drained the glass reservoir. He was replacing the hose when Hildy took her turn in the outhouse. Then she and Ruby dashed back into the cafe and came out with all the hamburgers wrapped in a newspaper.

"Soon's I refill my water bag," Seth informed them, "we'll be on our way. Umm! Them burgers smell mighty good. You boys start eatin' and then git back in the car."

He removed a canvas bag from the front bumper where air moving past it kept the water cool. After filling it from an outside garden hose coiled against the store, he replaced the bag on the bumper and walked around the car, inspecting the narrow tires. Then he slid under the wheel and took a hamburger from Hildy, who was again in the front seat.

He smiled at her. "Yore welcome to sleep up here if'n ye want, Hildy, but maybe it'd be more comfortable in back with Tom. I'm not gonna stop no more, jist drive straight through. I'll wake ye when we git thar."

That was good news to Hildy. She just hoped Seth didn't go to sleep at the wheel and have a wreck.

Hildy crawled into the back with Ruby. Each ate another hamburger and then wished for a drink of water, but Seth didn't stop. He drove on, steering the car with one hand and feeding himself with the other.

Hildy made herself as comfortable as possible and soon fell asleep beside Ruby.

Hours later, Hildy awakened to feel the car slowing. She opened her eyes to the coming of dawn and sat up slowly, aching in her neck and back from having slept curled up like a dog. Ruby still snored away on the backseat.

Hildy leaned forward. "Where are we?" she asked softly.

"That's the Blue River up yonder," Seth replied. "We're a-turnin' in at the Rockin' R Ranch whar ye said yore uncle works."

Excitement rose inside Hildy again. She touched her sleeping cousin lightly. "Ruby . . . uh . . . Tom, we're here."

Hildy glanced fearfully at Seth, but he gave no indication that he had noticed her slip. Ruby sat up slowly and yawned.

The Ford passed under an archway made of twelve-by-twelve timbers. A pair of longhorn steer horns about six feet in length was suspended above the ranch's name, which was spelled out with a piece of rope nailed to a weathered board.

Hildy's throat went suddenly dry. "You think Molly and the kids are here?" she whispered.

"Know in a minute," her cousin replied.

The long dirt drive curved slightly, and a ranch house loomed out of the dawn. In back of that, Hildy saw several outbuildings, including a barn and sheds. There were also some cabin-like structures. Hildy's blue eyes searched in vain for a truck or kids, although it was too early for her sisters and brother to be up.

Seth pointed ahead. "There's a feller a-ridin' a horse outta that thar corral," he announced. "Is that yore uncle?"

"I don't know. I've never met him."

The car's headlights showed a beefy man in cowboy clothing—a gray wide-brimmed hat with a seven-inch-high crown tapered in western style, faded blue jeans and jacket, and rough-side-out boots.

As the car chugged toward the man, Hildy saw that he was too old to be her uncle.

"Howdy," he said as Seth pulled up in front of him. The noisy car made the sorrel snort nervously and dance sideways, but the man had complete control. He had a very red, deeply lined face and long sideburns, which were sandy colored but probably had been bright red at one time. His paunch spilled over a huge silver belt buckle of a bucking horse.

"Howdy," Seth replied. "Yore name Cecil?"

The cowboy spoke soothingly to the horse before answering. "No. Cecil's in the barn," he said with a hint of a soft drawl.

Seth gestured to the backseat. "Them boys in back is his kin. We'd be obliged to see him."

The older man shifted in the saddle and Hildy caught a pleasant whiff of leather. "Cecil's feedin' his string," the rancher explained in his easy drawl. "Some of the horses ain't used to cars. Maybe you'd oughtta leave your Tin Lizzie here and walk over to see him."

Hildy couldn't wait any longer. "Is his sister and her children with him?" she blurted out.

The old man regarded Hildy thoughtfully before answering. "Why don't you ask him yourself?" The old cowboy turned away, guiding his horse toward the ranch house.

"Curmudgeon!" Hildy muttered as she climbed stiffly out of the backseat. It was the first time she had been able to use the word.

Ruby scowled. "What'd ye say?"

"Oh, nothing! I was just thinking of something Spud said."

Hildy, Ruby, and Seth hurried through the dusty yard to a barn. As soon as they entered, they heard horses stomping their hooves and munching feed from a long wooden trough.

Hildy spotted a stake-sided Reo truck parked in one corner of the barn. *That's what Molly and the kids must have ridden in from the Ozarks*, Hildy told herself.

Her heart speeded up as she heard a man's voice from behind the manger. "'Morning!"

Hildy and her two companions spun around toward the speaker. He was a short, wiry man with a black, high-crowned, tapered cowboy hat with a metal-studded leather band. The hat seemed too big for his small, sturdy body. He held a three-tined pitchfork in strong brown hands.

"Uncle Cecil?" Hildy asked, taking an uncertain step toward him.

For a second, the short cowboy stared silently at the three

visitors. Then he dropped the fork and strode forward. "I don't think I've had the pleasure," he said.

"I'm Hildy. Hildy Corrigan."

The cowboy stopped and cocked his head suspiciously. His deep brown eyes searched hers. "Hildy's a gal," he replied mildly.

"I'm Hildy," she repeated. Snatching off her cap, she let her brunette braids fall. "And she's Ruby." Hildy reached out and swept the cap off her cousin. "See?"

Uncle Cecil stared, his mouth open in surprise.

Seth took a half step backward and stared unbelievingly at the two passengers he had driven from the Ozarks. "I'm Seth Highton," he said, "and I swear to ye, Mister, I didn't know until this blessed second that these two ain't boys!"

Hildy brushed the confusion aside. "Are Molly and the kids here?"

Uncle Cecil clomped closer in his cowboy boots and peered carefully at the three visitors, then shook his head. "I'm sorry. No," he answered at last. "They went on to our parents' place in Illinois."

Hildy sagged weakly, and Seth automatically reached out and steadied her.

"I'm all right," she managed to say. She searched the short cowboy's face in hopes she had heard wrong. But she hadn't. She knew that. She had missed Molly and the kids.

Uncle Cecil patted her arm. "Come on over to the bunk-house. I'll rustle up some coffee and we can talk."

Wordlessly, and sick with her hopes crushed, Hildy trailed the cowboy and Seth out of the barn.

Ruby walked beside Hildy. "Don't ye fret none, Hildy," she whispered. "We'll find 'em yet."

Hildy tried to nod but wasn't very convincing. Molly and the kids were in Illinois. How could Hildy get to them?

Seth turned around and stared at the girls again. Walking backward, he spoke to Ruby. "So ye ain't really a Tom? Yore a Ruby?"

Ruby nodded silently.

"What's yore last name?"

"Konning," Ruby answered softly.

Seth nodded, turning around to walk with Hildy's Uncle Cecil.

The bunkhouse was where working cowboys lived. But the bunk beds lining the walls here were stripped to the frames. Only one lower one seemed to be in use. Uncle Cecil threw his hat on it, indicating the bunk was his. He explained that the Depression had forced the owner to lay off all the other ranch hands.

Cecil motioned for his guests to find seats while he made coffee. He placed a gray graniteware pot on top of a small pot-bellied stove, then filled it with water from a galvanized bucket and added scoops of coffee.

Hildy could hardly breathe. "Uncle Cecil, you said Molly and the kids went on to your parents' place in Illinois."

"Yep." He clamped the lid on the pot. "I put them on the motor stage for Foleyville yesterday morning. A couple of days before, my sister had telegraphed our folks that she was here. They wired back, insisting Molly visit them until their . . . *your* . . . . father gets there."

Hildy's heart thumped faster. "He's coming? When? How d'you know?"

The short cowboy chuckled and lifted the lid of the coffeepot with a calloused hand, dropping in an eggshell. "Settles the grounds down," he explained.

Hildy was annoyed by the delay.

"My sister talked to him in California by long distance telephone," Cecil finally continued. "He said that as soon as he could buy a car, he was leaving for Illinois. He plans on taking everyone back with him to the ranch where he works outside a little town called Lone River."

"I've got to get to Illinois before he does!" Hildy cried.

Cecil frowned. "I can't figure out why you came here, Hildy. Molly said you wanted to stay with your grandmother."

"That's not true. Please, how can Ruby and I get to Illinois fast?"

Cecil shrugged. "I don't rightly know. But maybe you could ask your father."

Hildy blinked, not understanding. "Ask him?"

"Telephone him long distance," Cecil explained. "Molly left me the number where he can be reached."

"Telephone?" Hildy asked.

"Yes, Hildy. You ever used a phone?"

"No, but I'll learn how—fast!"

Cecil chuckled. "I'll bet you will. Well, the nearest one's in town. Soon's I finish my chores, we'll drive in and see what we can do." Turning back to the stove, he lifted the lid from the pot. "Guess the coffee's ready," he said. "Everybody grab a cup off the shelf there."

Hildy impulsively reached out and embraced Ruby. "I'm going to talk to my daddy!" she cried happily. "Soon we'll all be together again!"

But would she?

CHAPTER
ELEVEN

MORE BAD NEWS

Seth Highton drained his tin coffee cup and stood up. "Well, I'd best be a-gittin' along. I wish ye well, Hildy. And you, too, Tom . . . I mean, Ruby."

Hildy got up from where she'd been sitting on an empty bunk bed in the sparsely furnished bunkhouse. "I can never thank you enough," she said quietly. "I wish there was some way I could repay you for your kindness to Ruby and me."

"Ye might say a little prayer so that Rachel don't throw me out fer jist showin' up like this," he said with a gentle smile.

"I will," Hildy assured him without thinking. She hadn't prayed much in a long, long time.

Seth rubbed his right hand along his stubbly black beard. "Got to find me a tourist cabin or somethin' an' clean up a mite. Then I'm a-goin' courtin' her."

"You don't have to go anyplace," Cecil said. "Use this bunkhouse to clean up. My straight edge razor's on the shelf there."

"Reckon mebby I will wash up," Seth replied. "Got me one of them new kind of safety razors an' a bar of soap in an old sock, so I'll shave and change clothes. Put on my Sunday-go-to-meetin' clothes. I bought me a gen-u-wine year-'round, one hundred percent virgin wool worsted suit for twelve dollars an' a half two years ago." He added a little sheepishly, "I ordered it by mail right outta the Sears an' Roebuck wish book."

"If I was you, I'd take a little nap, too," Cecil suggested. "Looks like you've not slept in a long time. Need to look your best to call on a lady, you know."

"But I cain't sleep 'til I know what Rachel's thinkin'," Seth protested.

Cecil nodded. "Suit yourself. I'll take the girls over and introduce them to the ranch owner and see if he'll let me drive them into town to make that phone call."

"If y'all be back by the time I'm ready, ye kin take my flivver if'n yore a mind to," Seth offered.

"Thanks," Cecil replied. "But that's not necessary. I could borrow the boss's truck—the one he let me use to pick up my sister and the kids in Arkansas—but I'd ruther take my own car. It's parked behind the tack room."

Hildy swept both men with an imploring look. "One thing first: would you mind not ever telling anybody about Ruby and me being girls?"

"I've been meaning to ask," Cecil said slowly. "What's the idea of the boys' get-up? You hiding from somebody?"

Hildy nodded. "Yes. A man named Vester Hardesty."

Seth made a startled sound. "I heerd tell of him. About the meanest man in the Ozarks. But . . . why's he after y'all?"

Hildy briefly explained.

"Neither Molly nor me knew that, Hildy!" Cecil exclaimed. "Otherwise, we'd never have left the Ozarks without you."

Hildy sighed. "I've got to straighten this all out with Molly. So I've got to talk to her before she and the kids leave for California . . . or Vester catches Ruby and me."

"Nobody's going to touch you while you're around me," Cecil said evenly.

"Nor me," Seth promised. "An' I won't tell nary a soul 'bout ye two bein' girls—'ceptin' Rachel. I don't want no secrets from her."

"You got my word, too," Cecil added.

Hildy and Ruby thanked the men, then asked Seth to let them know how his meeting with Rachel went. He agreed, and they parted.

Cecil led the girls, still in overalls but minus their caps, to the back door of the ranch house. The sorrel gelding they had seen the cowboy riding earlier was tied to a post in the ground just outside the door.

At Cecil's knock, the older man came out of the darkened interior of the house onto a large screened-in back porch. Hildy caught a whiff of bacon frying and suddenly realized how hungry she was.

The ranch owner wasn't wearing his hat. He had a bald streak running the entire length of his head, with two reddish-sandy wreaths of hair on both sides above his ears. His scalp was very pink.

He pushed the screen door open and blocked it with his scuffed cowboy boot.

Cecil spoke up. "Harold, this is my sister's oldest stepdaughter, Hildy Corrigan. You met the rest of the kids when they was here. Hildy just got in. Girls, this is my boss, Harold Witt."

Hildy smiled, saying, "Hello, Mr. Witt."

He nodded. "Hildy."

Cecil rested his hand on Ruby's shoulder. "This here's Ruby Konning, cousin to Hildy."

"Howdy," Ruby replied.

"Come in," the rancher said, holding the screen door open wider.

"No, thanks, Harold," Cecil told him. "I come to ask if it was okay for me to drive into town and phone Hildy's father in California. Through a misunderstanding, she stayed in the Ozarks with her granny when I picked up my sister and the other kids. But Hildy wants to join up with her stepmother and the rest of her family."

The rancher thoughtfully studied the girls with their boys' overalls and old work shirts.

Cecil noticed his concern. "I'll explain everything later, but I need to make that call right away. I oughtn't to be gone more'n an hour."

"Well," the old cowboy said in his soft drawl, "want to borry the Reo again?"

Cecil shook his head. "Much obliged anyway, but I'll take my car."

The rancher nodded and started to close the screen door, then stopped and frowned, looking thoughtfully at Ruby. "Did you say your last name was Konning?"

"Yes, sir."

"Is that spelled with a *C* or a *K*?"

"With a *K*."

"Konning," the rancher repeated. "Unusual name. Hmm. Sounds sort of familiar, but I can't place it. Oh, well, maybe it'll come to me."

As Cecil led the way toward the tack room, Ruby pulled on Hildy's arm. "What d'ye suppose he meant? Reckon he knew my pa?"

Hildy shrugged, unwilling to raise her cousin's hopes.

Cecil took off his hat to wipe his brow, then set it back on his head. "Lots of men drifted on and off this ranch since the Depression started, but I don't know's I ever met anybody by the name of Konning before."

Ruby sighed, but Hildy noticed a renewed hope in her cousin's face.

Cecil's car was parked under a corrugated metal roof attached to the back of the tack room. "This is a 1923 Gardner touring sedan," the small cowboy explained. "I bought it new at the factory for twelve hundred dollars. Traded in my Baby Overland because it was underpowered. This here's got four cylinders and two-wheel brakes, but she's old and not in very good shape anymore."

Hildy didn't really care about such things, but she listened politely and inspected the vehicle. It looked longer than Seth's Model T. The Gardner sedan had a black canvas top and four doors that only came up about waist high. There were no sides from there to the roof.

As the old vehicle started down the long dirt driveway, Cecil explained a strange clicking noise. "That's the wooden spokes in the wheels. The wood's all dried out. Every time a spoke comes to the top in a revolution, it's so loose it falls back into place. You'll get used to it. Makes a nice kind of rhythm."

Hildy wasn't really interested as long as the old car didn't break down. She switched the subject to her pressing concern. "I'll pay you for the telephone call soon's I can."

"Forget it, Hildy. Enjoy the ride."

The girl was too excited to really do that. Still, she glanced around as the Gardner touring car crunched onto the main sandy road that led toward town.

The Blue River was off to the right, Cecil explained. There was curly mesquite all around them as well as buffalo and grama grass, and lots of limestone. The whole area was a rolling prairie. No hill was more than a hundred feet high. "Compared to the Ozarks," Cecil remarked, "these aren't even foothills. More like toehills."

As the car neared the outskirts of the small ranching community called Big Bend, Hildy turned to her uncle. "Uncle Cecil, I've been doing some thinking. Ruby and I should put our boys' caps back on when we're in town. That way, if Vester shows up and asks anybody if they've seen two strange girls, people can say no. If they say they saw two boys, Vester probably won't figure out that it's us—at least, I hope not."

Before the wiry cowboy could answer, Ruby spoke. "There ain't no way Vester kin find us now. We rode in Seth's car clean out of the Ozarks and halfway acrosst Oklahoma. We's safe."

Hildy shook her head. "I know it may sound strange, Ruby, but I just don't want to take any chances. If we keep our boys' clothes on in town; then only Uncle Cecil, Seth, and Mr. Witt will know who we really are."

Cecil chuckled. "The way he was studying your clothes back there, you got him to wondering what's going on. But it don't make no never-mind to me if you want to look like boys again."

Ruby nodded. "Fine with me." She pulled her cap from the bib pocket of her overalls and put it on. Hildy did the same, tucking her braids carefully under the cap. Having completed that task, she began thinking what she wanted to say to her father.

By the time the touring car stopped in front of the drugstore, the only place with a public phone, Hildy was ready. She and Ruby followed Cecil as his cowboy boots made loud clomping sounds on the wooden floor. The store smelled of sawdust and cleaning fluid.

The druggist saw them heading for the green metal phone booth with a glass door. "Sorry, folks," he called, peering over the top of small round eyeglasses, "all the lines are down. No phones working anywhere around here at all. Be twenty-four hours before they're working again."

"Oh no," Hildy moaned. "Now what'll I do?"

Uncle Cecil frowned, then smiled. "Only other way is to send a telegram. Come on, I'll drive us to the depot. Hildy, you can only use ten words, so think of what you want to say."

The switch in plans was so sudden that it took Hildy a few minutes to work out in her mind what she could say in so few words. But by the time Cecil parked behind the train depot, Hildy knew what those words were.

The girls followed him around the long building and into a waiting room that smelled of age and stale cigar smoke. There was no one in the building. Its long wooden seats had shiny backs, polished by the restlessness of thousands of travelers. At the ends of the benches brass cuspidors stood ready for men who chewed tobacco.

"Trains don't stop here for passengers no more," Cecil explained. "Times is too hard for traveling by rail."

A bony old man, wearing a green visor, white shirt, black open vest and black armbands, peered at them through an iron grillwork. "Mornin', Mister. Boys."

"Morning," Cecil replied. "We'd like to send a telegram to California."

"I'm the telegrapher," the old man informed them, "so your wire'll go out right away. Take a sheet from one of those pads over there." He pointed to his right. "Write out your message, and bring it back to me when you're ready."

Ruby and Cecil followed as Hildy moved quickly to the pads, took one of the yellow sheets, and leaned over the high counter.

With a pencil stub tied to a small chain, she printed rapidly:

I'm at Cecil's heading for Molly's parents'. Wait for me.

The wiry cowboy counted the words and nodded. "That's fine. Only if I was your daddy, I'd be worried sick about what you're doing here, and how you're going to get to Illinois."

"What else can I do?"

"You could try phoning him again tomorrow."

"I want to be on my way to Illinois before then."

"I can't let you girls go on alone," Cecil protested. "You've got to wait to see if he answers your telegram."

The thought hadn't occurred to Hildy. "I can't do that!" she exclaimed, glancing helplessly at Ruby.

"You may have to," Cecil insisted, "because your father could already be on his way to Illinois. When Molly talked to him, he said he'd buy a car and start out soon's possible."

A wave of fear washed over Hildy. "When was that?"

"Let's see," Cecil said thoughtfully. "Molly talked to him about three days ago. She and the kids left yesterday. Figuring it might only take one day to buy a car, your father could have left California the day before yesterday."

Hildy's head reeled. "How long would it take him to drive?"

"I think he told Molly it was about twenty-five hundred miles, and he could do it in about five days."

"Five days?" Hildy exclaimed. "If he left two days ago, that could mean he's nearly halfway there!"

"That's true," Cecil agreed.

"But I've got to get to Illinois before he takes Molly and the kids back to California. Otherwise, I might never see them again!"

"Hildy," her uncle said sadly, "there's no way you can do that."

CHAPTER TWELVE

THE GATHERING STORM

I'll find a way!" Hildy almost shouted.

"Shhh!" Ruby whispered. "The man's looking at you."

Hildy glanced at the telegrapher, and he quickly glanced down to some papers on the desk behind the grillwork.

Hildy lowered her voice. "Uncle Cecil, how far is it from here to Foleyville?"

"Let's see—barely under eight hundred miles to Chicago, and just over five hundred miles to St. Louis. So Foleyville must be somewhere around six hundred miles from Big Bend."

"How long would it take if Ruby and I could go straight there?"

"That'd have to be by car. Figure thirty-five miles an hour tops is pretty good driving time. At maybe ten hours driving per day, that'd be three-hundred and fifty miles a day times two days—that's seven hundred miles. But since Foleyville's not quite that—"

"Then it could be done in two days," Hildy interrupted.

"Maybe, but the motor stage only goes once a week, and it's already gone for this week."

"Maybe we can get a ride with someone, like we did with Seth."

Cecil pushed his cowboy hat back on his head. "Be reasonable, Hildy," he protested. "I can't let you two go off alone like that."

"Uncle Cecil, we're going to Illinois, one way or another. And we're going to be there by the time my father arrives!"

She said it with such quiet conviction that the wiry cowboy sighed. "Let's get this telegram off and see what we can think of."

Hildy shoved her message under the iron grillwork to the telegrapher. "How long before we can expect an answer, Mister?" she asked.

"Come back about five o'clock tomorrow afternoon, Sonny."

"Tomor—? I can't wait that long!"

Ruby punched Hildy in the ribs. "Not now," she whispered under her breath.

It was all Hildy could do to keep her emotions under control while Cecil paid for the wire and the three walked back outside to the Gardner touring car. All the way back to the ranch, Hildy's mind twisted and turned with possibilities, but not one was practical.

Hildy's stomach knotted in anxiety as the Gardner turned off the sand onto the long dirt road leading to the ranch. Even from the arched gateway, Hildy could see that Seth Highton's Model T was gone. Apparently he had not taken a nap but had eagerly rushed off to see Rachel.

As the Gardner eased by the house, an older woman stepped out of the back screen door and hailed Cecil.

He slowed the car. "That's the boss's wife, Rebecca," he told Hildy and Ruby. "She's as fine a woman as ever drew breath." He applied the two-wheel brakes, and the car shuddered to a stop.

Mrs. Witt, wearing a long dark skirt, a short-sleeved light blue blouse, and a bright flowered apron tied about her waist, approached the car and looked at the girls. "My husband told me we had company."

"Yes, ma'am," Cecil replied. "This here's my sister's step-daughter, Hildy Corrigan, and her cousin, Ruby Konning. They got separated from their family, and we're trying to get them all back together again."

Everyone exchanged greetings while Hildy studied Mrs. Witt. She was short, somewhat stout, with skin darker than a tan. Her black hair showed just a few strands of gray. Hildy guessed there was some Indian blood a few generations back in Mrs. Witt's family.

The rancher's wife spoke with motherly concern. "Harold just told me about you traveling all night. Have you had break-fast?"

Cecil smacked his forehead lightly with his right hand. "Aw, Miz Witt, since I always eat so early, I didn't think about whether they had or not. Have you, girls?"

The mention of food magnified the painful emptiness in Hil-dy's stomach. She and Ruby hadn't eaten anything since the two nickel hamburgers the night before. Still, she didn't want to impose on the boss's wife because Mr. Witt had allowed Uncle Cecil time off to drive into town.

Ruby, however, didn't stand on formality. "We ain't et in a coon's age!" she blurted.

"That's what I thought." The older woman nodded with sat-isfaction. "You men are all alike. My husband stood there talking to you a while ago when I was getting his breakfast. I imagine the smell of that bacon must have made you girls powerful hun-gry. Now come on. Get out of that car and follow me."

Hildy and Ruby glanced at Uncle Cecil.

He nodded. "I'll put the car away and get on with my chores."

Hildy didn't want to waste any time starting for Illinois, but she realized her stomachache was only partly from anxiety. Some of it was from hunger. She and Ruby followed Mrs. Witt across the back porch and into the large, open kitchen with windows on two sides. Hildy glimpsed lots of deep cupboards, a huge cast-iron wood stove, and a small table with sturdy chairs. A hand-pump handle at the sink meant the Witts had running water.

Ruby gazed in open-mouthed wonder. "I ain't never seen nothin' like this afore!"

"It's nice," Hildy agreed. "Real nice, Mrs. Witt." To Hildy, it really felt like a home.

"Needs a little touchin' up," the woman replied, glancing around at the cracked, peeling wall paint. "But until this Depression ends, we'll make do, like everybody else does."

Hildy heard a chirp and looked into the far corner of the kitchen. A yellow canary inside a cage cocked his head while his bright eyes studied the two girls.

"Oh, how pretty!" Hildy exclaimed. "I've never seen a bird like this."

"He's a canary. Name's Lindy," Mrs. Witt said, taking a pan from a peg beside the stove. "Our girls named him that. All five are grown and married now."

Ruby walked closer to the cage to look. "We know a boy who named his dog Lindy," she said.

Hildy suddenly felt sad, wondering where their friend Spud and his dog were.

Mrs. Witt set a pan on the stove top. "My husband says everybody in this county has a horse, dog, mule, or something named Lindy. That Lindbergh fellow sure has lots of namesakes these days. Well, why don't you two wash up while I fix something to eat?"

She pointed through the open door to the living room. "Go through there and down the hallway. First door on the right. My husband installed indoor plumbing just before the stock market crash when everybody's money troubles started."

The girls started out of the kitchen; then Ruby turned back. "Oh, Miz Witt, yore husbun' mentioned a while ago that he thought he knew the name Konning." She smiled hopefully. "Do you remember it?"

The woman shook her head and pursed her lips. "Can't say's I do. Still, it does have a familiar ring to it. I'll ask Harold when I get a chance."

Ruby's smile faded as she joined Hildy in the rug-covered, dark hallway. As they passed the open door to the big parlor, they saw Indian blankets, cowhide chairs, and coal-oil lamps mounted on wall brackets. The flowered, cream-colored wall-paper was peeling, and on the fireplace mantel, sepia-tone pho-tographs of five girls rested in oval frames.

Hildy and Ruby stopped just outside the bathroom. They had never seen one before, but it was full of marvelous things. To the right, a large frosted window admitted sunlight. For girls whose only baths had been in a washtub or a pan of water, the glistening white bathtub under the window intrigued them. The tub's four short, curved legs ended in giant talons, each one gripping a large glass ball that rested on the linoleum.

Straight ahead, there was a small pump with a short handle above a basin built into a vanity. On the wall behind the pump a huge mirror extended from the vanity to the ceiling. On both sides of the basin, a dozen or more tiny perfume or cologne bottles and small dusting powder containers stood in neat rows. Their reflection in the mirror seemed to double the sizes.

Hildy eased forward and carefully sniffed a vial, closing her eyes. "Smells wonderful!" she exclaimed. Then she checked the fragrance of two other bottles. "Ruby, I'm going to have one of these rooms someday," she said. "It'll be part of our family's 'forever home.' "

"Ye won't if'n ye don't git to Foleyville in time." Ruby tilted her chin up to gaze at something mounted against the left wall about six feet up. "Wonder what this here thing is fer? Looks like a tank. Got a chain hangin' down with a little wooden han-dle. See?"

She reached out impulsively and gave it a pull. Instantly there was a sound of rushing water. Both girls jumped back in surprise as a white bowl-like object on the floor gushed with swirling water. It rose alarmingly as though it were going to overflow on the linoleum.

"Now you've done it!" Hildy cried.

"I didn't mean to!" Ruby wailed.

"We'd better go tell Mrs. Witt we broke it—whatever it is,"

Hildy said. "I just hope we can do enough work around here to pay for it."

As the cousins turned to leave the bathroom, the water quieted down. Slowly, barely daring to hope, they swung around to examine the strange sight. The white bowl on the floor no longer threatened to overflow. There was only the muted sound of water running into the high overhead tank. As the girls stood in hopeful silence, even that noise stopped.

"You know what this must be?" Hildy whispered.

"Yeah," Ruby whispered back. "But I never knowed one could be inside the house."

The girls returned to the kitchen and sat down to a huge breakfast of pork chops, eggs, biscuits, and country gravy with sausage chunks.

Mrs. Witt poured some water for the girls. "We haven't had any milk since our last daughter moved away and we sold our cow," she apologized. "The kids' last dog died a few months ago, so it's just Harold and me now—and Cecil. He's a mighty good all-around hand."

Setting down the water pitcher, she sat down across the table from the girls. "I'll say a table grace for you if you'd like," she offered. Then without waiting for an answer, she began praying the nicest prayer Hildy had ever heard. Mrs. Witt talked to God as if He were sitting right there with them at the table. She thanked Him for providing the food and asked for help in reuniting Hildy with her family.

When the girls looked up from the prayer, Mrs. Witt smiled and began making small talk. Their hostess discussed the weather and things on the ranch but seemed to deliberately avoid asking personal questions about her guests. Hildy supposed that was part of the western code—mind your own business. Her husband had implied that when he refused to answer questions about Cecil when the girls first arrived. Hildy felt it best to say nothing about her problem, and Ruby seemed to feel the same way.

After a few minutes, Mrs. Witt got up to check more biscuits in the oven. "We never had us a son, so our girls kind of grew up like tomboys. You two can sleep in one of their rooms tonight."

Hildy swallowed. "Thanks, Mrs. Witt," she said politely, "but we'll be on our way before then."

The woman turned around quickly and straightened up. But before she could say anything, her husband clomped across the back porch in his cowboy boots and stuck his head in the door.

"If you two are through eating, you'd better come with me before Rebecca puts you to work washing dishes or something."

"We'd be glad to wash dishes or anything else," Hildy answered.

"Well, come on outside anyway," the rancher grinned. "I want you both to see my horse, Blaze."

"Oh, I love horses!" Hildy exclaimed. "Ruby and I used to ride our neighbor's horses quite a bit back home in Possum Hollow."

"Well, that's fine," Mr. Witt replied. "Now, Hildy, Cecil's got a gentle mare he wants you to try. He says if you two can ride well enough, he'll let you move a small herd tomorrow afternoon. He'll go into town to see if there's an answer to your telegram."

Hildy spoke with controlled patience. "Mr. Witt, we'll not be here tomorrow. We've got to start for Molly's parents' place right away."

"Girls, Cecil's told me about your problems," the rancher drawled. "Why not give us grownups a little while to think about it? We'll try to find a way to help you."

He didn't wait for an answer but turned to his wife. "Rebecca, they'll need boots and pants. See if some of those our girls left will fit these girls."

Mrs. Witt showed them the nearest daughter's bedroom and told the girls to help themselves to anything in the closet. Then she left the room.

Hildy muttered under her breath. "We're going horseback riding while Vester's getting closer and my father's about to take the family off to California!"

"Hildy, these nice people are a-tryin' to he'p us!" Ruby

snapped. "Since we ain't got no idee on how to git to Illinois, hesh up an' git dressed."

When the girls had found old ranch-style clothes that fit reasonably well, they hurried outside to where Mr. Witt and Cecil were waiting.

"This is Blaze," the rancher said, patting the sturdy neck of his sorrel gelding. "Best cow pony around. You can both try him if you want."

When the girls had taken turns riding around the corral, the men seemed satisfied.

Mr. Witt slapped his ranch hand on the back. "Cecil, why don't you take our young friends with you to move that herd to fresh pasture? Ruby, you may's well stay on my horse. Hildy, you'll like Blackie, the little mare Cecil picked out for you."

Hildy started to protest, but Ruby whispered, "Wait fer yore father's telegram tomorry. Then we'll head for Illinois."

Hildy sighed. "One more day, but that's all." She glanced at the sky and sighed again. A storm was coming. *Nothing's going right!* she thought.

She felt so helpless. Suddenly she wished she could pray like Mrs. Witt.

CHAPTER THIRTEEN

THE STORM BREAKS

Hildy mounted Blackie and reined her over beside Cecil on his big bay gelding while Ruby adjusted her position on Mr. Witt's sorrel. Cecil took the lead as the three rode past the barn to a sturdy side corral. Leaning over from his saddle, he opened a wooden gate.

All three cow ponies knew what to do. Without any urging, the mare and geldings quietly moved about twenty head of horned cattle through the gate. As the cattle started toward the open prairie, the girls swung their mounts along either side of the wiry cowboy.

Hildy glanced at the sky again. "Looks like a thunder shower coming up."

Ruby grinned. "Ye won't rust!"

Cecil rode easily, reins lightly held in his left hand. "Typical late afternoon thunder and lightning show for this time of year," he said. "It'll pass fast. But I brought slickers. Here—better put them on."

The girls rode closer to Cecil, and he handed each a black poncho-like garment. All three donned the rain gear as the thunder rumbled closer and the lightning lit up the blackened sky.

As they rode on, soon the ranch fell behind. Only curly mesquite and a vast expanse of grama and buffalo grass stretched in an endless, rolling sea.

Hildy trained her eyes on the horizon. "Nothing out here but miles and miles of nothing," she remarked.

"Can get kinda lonesome," Cecil admitted. "But there's life out here. I sometimes see a red wolf, but there are no more gray lobos left. You never want to be afoot out here," he warned. "So if you do get off your horse for any reason, never let go the reins. If the horse runs off, it's a powerful long walk back."

The storm boomed louder and closer, making conversation difficult. One very black cloud moved in fast, and an ominous gloom spread over the land. Lightning split the dark sky with long, jagged streaks. Thunderclaps followed hard, then faded away into the distance.

Hildy had experienced thunderstorms all her life, yet this one was different. There was something scary about being so far from any sign of a building. There were only the hills, the endless sea of waving grass, and the storm.

She looked ahead at the cattle. They were still moving, apparently unconcerned about the storm. Suddenly, Hildy's eyes opened wide in surprise. Streaks of electricity leaped from horn to horn throughout the herd.

"What's that?" she asked in alarm.

Cecil raised his voice above the storm. "Don't rightly know, but I've seen that lots of times. Harold says it's static electricity. To me, it looks sort of like lightning jumping from their horns."

He waited until a clap of thunder rolled off into the distance, then lightly reined in his horse. "I think the heat of their bodies draws it. The cattle don't seem to feel it, but I always stay away from them."

Hildy and Ruby dropped back from the cattle, and all three riders stayed away from the livestock until they reached the other pasture. The rain fell hard as Cecil opened the gate, helped the girls drive the cattle through, then closed the gate again.

But the storm passed as quickly as it had come, and Cecil and the girls turned back to the ranch as the sky cleared. At the

corral, they stripped bridles, saddles, and blankets from the glis-
tening-wet animals.

About that time the old rancher came out of the barn carrying
a bridle. "You girls think you can handle a herd like that yourselves tomorrow?" he asked.

"Shore," Ruby replied confidently.

Hildy reluctantly nodded.

"Good," Mr. Witt drawled in approval. "You'll get a chance
when Cecil rides into town to see if an answer came to your
telegram."

At dinner, the girls told the Witts and Cecil the whole story
about how Hildy had been abandoned. The adults were sym-
pathetic but couldn't immediately come up with any solution.

"Too bad there's not one of those new airports around here,"
the rancher mused. "I hear they've got a passenger plane that
goes three miles a minute. Imagine that—a hundred and eighty
miles an hour!"

His wife stared down at her folded hands on the table.
"There's no train anymore, and no stage until next week," she
said grimly. "If we had the money, we'd maybe hire somebody
to take you girls in a car. But we're barely able to hang on to this
place as it is."

Hildy fidgeted in her chair. "We thank you for what you're
trying to do, but time's getting away from us," she said in des-
peration.

Cecil put his hand on her shoulder. "You two can't leave
here like you did in the Ozarks. If anything happened to you,
I'd never forgive myself," he told them. "Neither would your
father or my sister."

Mr. Witt stifled a yawn. "The best thing would be if we could
talk to your father, Hildy. Barring that, we need his answer to
your telegram." He pushed back his chair and stood. "Well, let's
all get some sleep. Maybe we'll think of something by morning."

Mrs. Witt showed Hildy and Ruby to a high-ceilinged room
with a massive four-poster bed. This bedroom had been their
youngest daughter's, she told them. Then she found them some
extra nightclothes to sleep in.

Ruby soon fell asleep, but Hildy lay awake a long time, thinking.

All her problems seemed to drop heavily upon her chest until she could barely breathe. It was true that complete strangers had helped her and been kind to her, but everywhere she had turned, frustration and more problems had popped up. Helplessness engulfed her like the black blanket of storm clouds they had encountered that afternoon. Not even the adults had been able to offer hope or a solution.

Hildy needed a strength and wisdom greater than her own, like the help Mrs. Witt asked for in her prayer that morning. Hildy sighed deeply, remembering a hymn her mother used to sing. The melody and the words drifted through her mind like a refreshing breeze. "Sweet hour of prayer. . . ."

Hildy suddenly remembered that she had promised Seth she would pray for him and Rachel. Hildy hadn't really prayed since her mother died, but she had promised Seth. Staring at the darkened ceiling, her lips moved. "Lord, thanks for Seth and the ride he gave us. Help him with his old sweetheart, please. Amen."

Her obligation completed, Hildy's thoughts leap-frogged about. She felt the gnawing pain of doubt and greater frustration.

I sure hope Daddy's telegram is there tomorrow or I can phone him—if he hasn't already started for Illinois. We've got to get there ahead of him so I can talk to Molly. I wonder what she'll say? What will the kids say? How can I get there?

Hildy's thoughts drifted to Granny. *I don't think I can ever forgive her*, Hildy thought angrily. *Especially for putting Vester on my trail. Oh, well, we've lost him now—I hope.*

Suddenly, Hildy sat bolt upright in the darkness, her heart pounding with a wild thought. *Granny must have told Vester I'd likely go to Uncle Cecil's. So even if Vester lost our trail, sooner or later he'll come here. Maybe he's here already!*

Hildy's sudden move woke Ruby, and she sat up, too. Then Hildy shared her latest fear with her cousin.

Ruby looked at her with wide, frightened eyes. "Yore right,

Hildy. We shoulda thought of that right off. Vester'll show up here, for shore."

"Oh, Ruby, why does everything go from bad to worse?"

"Maybe it'll git better when yore daddy's telegram comes tomorry."

Just then Mrs. Witt passed by their doorway with a coal-oil lamp. She stopped and peeked in, shielding the lamp with her free hand so the light wouldn't hit the girls in the face if they were asleep.

Mrs. Witt asked, "You girls all right?"

Hildy didn't know what to say. She couldn't lie, but she didn't want to bother Mrs. Witt anymore this late at night.

The rancher's wife seemed to sense the cousins' fears. "I always used to pray with my girls every night," she said. "I kind of miss it since they're all grown and gone. Would you let me pray with you two tonight?"

Ruby didn't say anything, but Hildy agreed after only a slight hesitation.

As Mrs. Witt knelt in her pink chenille robe beside the four-poster bed, she reached out and grasped the girls' hands. And then as Hildy closed her eyes, the woman began talking to God about the girls' scary situation and asking for His help in finding a solution. "Calm their hearts now, Lord, and help them sleep well, I pray, in Jesus' Name. Amen."

After a quick hug for them both, Mrs. Witt got up and headed back down the hall.

Although Hildy did feel a little better, she still lay awake for quite a while. But knowing there was nothing she could do until morning, she finally drifted off to sleep.

The next morning while the girls were dressing in the bathroom, they again discussed the telegram Hildy was waiting for. "D'ye think it'll come today?" Ruby asked.

"Let's hope so. But it'll be a long day until Cecil gets back from town this afternoon."

It was probably the longest, slowest day of Hildy's life. She and Ruby worked hard, helping Mrs. Witt with the household chores until she insisted they stop.

THE STORM BREAKS

The girls then saddled up to help Cecil and Mr. Witt around the ranch. Finally, it was time for Cecil to drive back into town to check on the telegram. By then, Hildy was as tense as a banjo's strings at a hoedown.

"Hurry back," she told Cecil as he slid into the front seat of the Gardner touring car.

He squinted at the sky. "Looks like another thunderstorm may be coming in. You and Ruby sure you can handle that herd by yourselves?"

"We're sure," Hildy replied.

She watched the car crunch down the long driveway. After the vehicle disappeared, the girls put on their slickers and again rode across the lonely prairie. Within half an hour, they found a herd of a dozen animals and began moving them toward another pasture.

The fast-moving storm swooped overhead in a mass of dark, threatening clouds, rapid lightning, and booming thunderclaps. Rain fell so hard that the girls could hardly see just a few feet in front of them. Hildy hoped the storm would pass as quickly as the one the day before.

Blackie and Blaze knew their duties so well that the girls hunched low over over the saddle horns against the driving rain and gave the horses slack rein.

Again the strange zigzag streaks of electricity jumped from the horns of the cattle. So both girls dropped back from the herd, remembering Cecil's belief that the animals' body warmth might attract the electric charges.

"This storm is even blacker than yesterday's," Hildy called to Ruby between crashes of thunder. "And look! Those little lightning streaks around the animals' heads give off a weird glow against this gloomy sky."

"Kinda scary," Ruby replied.

As the two horses plodded along, moving the herd slowly through the storm, the vast emptiness totally engulfed Hildy. "Mighty lonesome country," she called to Ruby.

Ruby peered through the driving rain and nodded, throwing water from the brim of her borrowed hat. "Shore hate to be afoot out here."

"Me, too."

That's when it happened. One moment Blackie was walking along at an easy pace. The next moment with a toss of her head and a jingling of metal, she was down. The mare collapsed hard without warning.

Hildy felt the horse falling and jerked her feet from the stirrups. She was still in the saddle, her boot heels touching the ground, when a tremendous clap of thunder boomed overhead. "Ruby!" she called, her heart thumping wildly.

Hildy half suspected lightning, but she hadn't seen anything. And she didn't feel anything. Whatever had happened affected only Blackie, leaving the mare sprawled on the ground in an awkward position. Her head lay in the grass, the rain bouncing off her extended neck. Her forefeet buckled under, but her hind legs were thrust out straight.

As Ruby rode her horse over to her cousin's side, Hildy still wasn't sure what had happened. Hildy pushed herself from the saddle and took a couple of quick steps toward Blackie's head. At first she thought the horse was dead, but still she automatically reached for the bridle, remembering what Cecil had said about the dangers of having to walk home.

But Blackie wasn't moving. The mare lay in a crumpled heap. Hildy's hands found the bridle in the driving rain just as the horse's head swung up.

Blackie whinnied and struggled to stand. She made it, but her legs were spread wide. She trembled all over.

Startled by the sudden movement, Blaze backed away nervously. Ruby spoke to him gently and reined him in closer. "What happened?" she asked, looking down at her cousin.

"I don't know." Hildy reached up and took the reins, swinging them over Blackie's neck and head. As she held the reins and backed off to examine the horse, she stepped on something and heard the clink of metal. She glanced down.

"Look! Those are her shoes. Blackie's lost a couple of shoes!" Hildy gasped, then barely breathed the words, "Blackie was hit by lightning!"

Ruby leaned down from Blaze's saddle to see better by the

flashes of lightning. "Shore was. She's plumb barefooted in front. Her shoes been knocked clean off!"

"The metal in the bit and shoes must have made the lightning go right through her."

"It's a miracle she weren't kilt outright. How 'bout you? Ye hurt?"

Hildy quickly looked over her body, moving her arms and legs. As the rain poured over her, she found that she could move normally. But the horse still trembled on wide-spread legs.

"No, I'm all right." Lightning continued to flash about them and thunder boomed unceasingly. Hildy glanced up. "Ruby!" she yelled in sudden fright. "You're the tallest thing out there now. Get down before you get hit, too!"

Ruby leaped from her horse's back onto the muddy wet grass, her eyes wide with fear. She held tightly to the reins but stood well away from the sorrel.

Hildy glanced again at the two metal horseshoes on the ground. The girl bent and carefully lifted each of Blackie's legs in turn, checking all four hooves.

Ruby, standing close, exclaimed, "Jist a couple nails left in that left front hoof, and look! The heads is burned right off them nails."

Hildy straightened, anxiously looking at the sky. The storm was moving quickly away. "I guess the saddle protected me," she mused, "and not having any metal touching the ground."

Instantly, the reality of what had happened hit Hildy with the suddenness of the lightning bolt she had not seen or felt. "I . . . I could have been killed!"

"Shore could've!" Ruby agreed.

For a moment, both girls were silent.

Finally Ruby broke the silence. "Well, you cain't ride Blackie with them nails a-stickin' out of her hoof. I reckon we'll jist have to leave her fer now. You ride double with me back to the ranch."

Hildy didn't seem to hear. Her mind leaped back to the night before when she had thought about Granny, when she had decided that she could never forgive the old woman for the things she had done. Guilt flooded through Hildy. What if she had died with that resentment and anger still inside?

Ruby tried to get her cousin's attention. "What's the matter with ye, Hildy? You shore ye didn't get hit by that lightnin', too?"

"I'm all right," Hildy said thoughtfully. She stripped bridle, saddle and blanket from the horse and dropped them on the grass. Hildy swung up behind Ruby and repeated, "I'm all right."

But she wasn't. All the way back to the ranch house, she was lost in deep thought. *I could have been killed!*

The sorrel, carrying double, approached the ranch at dusk. Hildy saw the silhouette of a car between the barn and house. She started to say that Cecil was back, but another look made her realize that she wasn't seeing the old Gardner touring car.

"Vester!" she whispered in sudden fear.

CHAPTER
FOURTEEN

HOPE IN A LONG, DARK NIGHT

Ruby shook her head. "Naw, that's Seth's Model T. Ye reckon he done brung his gal?"

"Maybe." Hildy's heart began to slow down from the sudden leap it had taken when she thought Vester's car was parked in the drive.

Hildy consciously tried to calm down as she helped Ruby strip the saddle, blankets, and bridle from the sorrel. Then after they turned him into the corral, they raced across the muddy driveway, scraped their boots at the back porch door, and hurried into the kitchen.

Mr. and Mrs. Witt sat at the table drinking coffee with Seth Highton and a pretty young woman wearing a bright pink dress. The mountaineer who had driven the girls from the Ozarks to the ranch was clean-shaven and wearing his twelve-dollar suit.

He grinned and stood up. "Howdy, Hildy and Ruby. This here's Rachel." He looked down with pride at the woman whose hair was black as a crow's wing in spring. "Honey, this here's the two gals I tol' ye 'bout."

Rachel smiled warmly and nodded. "I'm right glad to know you both." She was rather tall and slender with gray eyes.

Hildy smiled back and then turned to the rancher. "Mr. Witt, something terrible happened. Blackie got hit by lightning! But I think she's all right."

The adults reacted with concern.

Sitting down at the table, Hildy quickly reported the details while Ruby shifted restlessly from foot to foot. Finally Hildy concluded her story, "So we left her and rode double on your horse to come back here."

The rancher lifted a freckled hand to the bald streak on his head. "I'm glad you girls are all right. And it sounds as if Blackie'll be fine, too. Cecil and I will go bring her in first thing tomorrow."

When at last the incident with Blackie was resolved, Ruby looked across the table at Seth and Rachel and asked bluntly, "Seth, are the two of ye a-goin' to git hitched?"

Before the mountaineer could answer, headlights hit the kitchen window. Hildy jumped up. "That'll be Cecil with a telegram from my daddy!"

As she ran outside, the touring car's headlights picked her up, and the car stopped with the squealing of brakes. Hildy dashed out of the lights toward the driver's side. "You got the telegram?"

The cowboy's big hat seemed to fill the darkened interior of the car so Hildy couldn't see Cecil's face. He evaded her question. "I see your friend Seth's Model T is back. Did he bring his girl?"

"Yes, but what about Daddy's telegram?"

"It didn't come."

"You sure?"

"I'm sorry, Hildy. Maybe tomorrow."

Hildy felt suddenly sick. "Oh," she said in a whisper. She turned her face into the darkness so Cecil couldn't see the anguish on her face.

His voice came quietly from behind her. "There's something else, Hildy."

She swung around to face Cecil, sensing bad news.

"The telegraph operator told me that a stranger with a reddish beard and a pock-marked face came in this afternoon," Cecil explained. "He was looking for two girls."

"Vester! He's already here?"

"Looks that way, Hildy. Only good thing is that he's looking for girls—strangers in town. The operator told him he hadn't seen any."

Hildy felt a surge of relief that she and Ruby had worn their boys' disguises into town the day before.

"But," Cecil added, "the telegrapher told the pock-marked man that he had seen a couple of strange boys. Sooner or later, Vester will realize it was really you and Ruby."

Hildy nodded. "Last night I figured out that Granny must have told Vester about you and this ranch. So he would have come here eventually, even without the telegraph operator's help."

"Don't you worry, Hildy. This Vester person won't dare come on the ranch as long as you and Ruby are with Harold or me."

"I'm not so sure about that!" Hildy exclaimed.

"Let me put this car away," Cecil stated; "then I'll come inside so we can discuss it. And I want to meet Seth's lady friend, too."

Hildy turned and went back into the kitchen. "Daddy's telegram didn't come, and Vester's in town!" she blurted out.

That information plunged everyone into somber discussions. For the next few hours, they all tried to think of a way to get Hildy and Ruby to Illinois as soon as possible. However, the evening ended as it had the night before—without a solution.

After Seth and Rachel said good night and drove off, Cecil headed for the bunkhouse.

As Mrs. Witt washed out the coffee cups, her husband tried to reassure the girls. "We'll take a fresh look at this situation in the morning. You girls will be safe tonight," he promised. "So don't worry. Now, let's all get some sleep."

Mrs. Witt dried her hands carefully, then lit a lamp and carried it down the long dark hallway. The girls followed. Hildy watched the shadows slink away from the advancing light. But as the light passed, the shadows slipped silently in behind the girls. Hildy shivered, although she wasn't cold.

Setting the lamp on a white marble-topped night stand in the room the girls shared, the woman pulled the green shades on the single large window.

There was a faint scratching on the pane.

"What's that?" Hildy gasped, turning in fright toward the sound.

Mrs. Witt smiled. "That's only the branches from a tree that's grown too close to the house. I'll have them pruned back."

To Hildy it sounded like bony fingers probing for a way into the big room. She jumped up backward onto the high four-poster bed with massive, dark wooden head and footboards. Her feet dangled well off the rug as she began to unbraid her hair and brush it out with the brush she had brought in her tow sack. "Are you going to pray with us again tonight?" she asked the rancher's wife softly.

"I'd like that." Mrs. Witt smiled.

Both girls undressed quickly and slid under the top sheet. After a short but soothing prayer asking the Lord once again to help Hildy find her family, Mrs. Witt tucked the girls in with motherly concern. She picked up the lamp. "Good night," she murmured with a smile. "Please don't worry."

Hildy wanted to ask her to leave the lamp. *No, I'm too big for that*, she reminded herself.

When Mrs. Witt left, shadows instantly leaped into the room like living things. And as the light moved down the hallway toward the kitchen, the scary shadows in the bedroom gathered into a solid black mass. Hildy couldn't see her hand in front of her face, and her heart began to pound.

She tried to get control of her emotions. *Common sense says even Vester wouldn't be foolish enough to bother us now*, she told herself. *But I sure wish the Witts' dog hadn't died. It'd be nice to have one to bark if anyone came sneaking around.*

Hildy stared silently at the darkened ceiling a while. Finally she asked softly, "Ruby, you awake?"

"Uh huh."

"Vester'll keep trying, you know."

"I know." Then Ruby changed the subject. "Did ye hear that Seth and Rachel plan to git married?"

"Really? I was so upset about the telegram and Vester being in town, I forgot everything else."

For a moment, Hildy wondered if her dutiful sentence prayer on Seth's behalf had done any good. Or would Seth and Rachel have gotten together anyway?

Hildy's thoughts spun off again. Suddenly she sat upright in bed. "I know what! Tomorrow, if nobody comes up with a good way for us to get to Illinois, I'm going to try to telephone Daddy again. If he's not there, I'll talk to the people where he works. They'll know whether he's left or not, and how long ago."

"That's a good idee."

"If he's left California," Hildy added, "then we'll know how long we've got for getting to Foleyville before he does."

"What if it's too late?"

"Then we'll follow them back to California."

"That's crazy, Hildy. The longer we's out in the open, the sooner Vester's goin' to catch us!"

"He won't catch us. We can't let him!"

"That thar's foolish talk, and ye know it."

Hildy lay quietly for a moment in the darkness. She knew Ruby was right. Hildy's feelings of frustration, fear, and utter helplessness grew bigger.

After a long silence, Ruby whispered, "I'm skeered."

"Me, too." Hildy thought of the sudden way that Blackie had fallen when hit by lightning. She knew she could also have been struck and possibly killed. Hildy spoke softly into the darkness. "Ruby, I need forgiveness for the way I've felt about Granny."

"Why?" Ruby asked. "People been a-hurtin' me since I was borned, an' not one ever asked me fer no fergiveness."

Hildy knew that was true. Granny had also been mean to Ruby. Finally Hildy said into the darkness, "I'm going to write her soon's I can and say I'm sorry."

"A lotta good that'll do ye."

"I'm not responsible for what she does, Ruby—only what I do."

"Next thing ye know, y'all be askin' God's fergiveness too," Ruby said scornfully.

Hildy didn't answer. Up until she met Mrs. Witt, she would have said, *Why should I ask His forgiveness? Didn't He let my mother die when I prayed so hard for her to live?* But Mrs. Witt's prayers made the Lord sound so loving and caring, like someone you wouldn't want to hurt.

Hildy forced her thoughts back to Granny. "I don't want to hate her. I'm sorry for what I said to her. I'm sorry I ran off, too. Maybe she feels like I did when Molly ran off and left me."

"What are ye gonna do, Hildy?"

That's a good question, Hildy thought. "Well, after I write and say I love her, maybe I can come visit her someday."

"What if Vester grabs us afore we reach Molly's place?"

"We can't let that happen."

"How're ye gonna stop it? We know he's in town, and he'll be a-watchin' this place. Soon's we set foot off'n it, he'll be on us like an ol' hawk on baby chicks."

Hildy knew that was true. Uncle Cecil and Mr. Witt could protect the girls only while they remained under the men's care. But they could not stay here. They had to go on, and soon.

What we need, she thought, *is someone greater than Ruby or I or anyone we know. Someone stronger and wiser. Someone—*

Her thoughts snapped off and she gazed upward. "Someone . . . like God," she finished silently.

Immediately the doubts returned. *But He let me down. He let my mother die. He left all of us kids without a mother, and Daddy always off looking for work.*

A sentence popped into Hildy's head, something she had learned a long time before in the little log church at Possum Hollow: "I will never leave thee, nor forsake thee." *That's the kind of God Mrs. Witt knows*, Hildy thought.

But He did leave me! He let me down! He . . . Her thoughts trailed off as tears sprang to her eyes. She fought back sobs.

Did He?

The two words seemed to hang in front of her eyes so she could read them clearly, even in the darkness.

She lay quietly for a long time, her mind torn with doubts and a yearning for something greater than her own strength. At last she looked again at the ceiling through misty eyes. Her lips moved silently. "I'm . . . sorry."

That was all. Yet scalding tears gushed unbidden from her eyes and slid down her cheeks. She stifled her sobs so Ruby couldn't hear, but Hildy's body shook.

She didn't know how long that lasted, but at last she sniffed, blinked rapidly in the darkness and took a slow, deep breath. She let it out in a long, shuddering sigh of relief.

Then she slept. It was the first restful sleep she'd had in a long time.

At dawn, Hildy awoke to Cecil's angry shouts outside the house. "Stand still, I said! Get your hands up!"

"Vester!" Hildy exclaimed, leaping out of bed. "Ruby, Cecil's caught him!"

The girls hastily pulled on dresses Mrs. Witt had laid out for them, then rushed through the house and out the back porch.

Mr. Witt was riding his sorrel toward the barn, where Cecil held a three-tined pitchfork toward a person barely visible in the first light of day.

The girls ran side-by-side across the open yard toward Cecil and his prisoner. Hildy expected to see Vester's pocked face and heavyset body. Instead, she saw a boy and a dog.

"Spud!" Hildy cried. "And Lindy!"

The Airedale's short, wiry black and tan hair stood straight up along his neck. He growled, hackles raised, standing stiff-legged, facing Cecil, ready to attack. But firm commands from Spud kept him in check.

Ruby slowed and stopped. "I thought we was shed of him," she said.

Hildy ran on, calling over her shoulder, "You be nice to him!"

The taller girl muttered, "I should have whupped him whilst

I had the chance't back in the Ozarks."

"Uncle Cecil!" Hildy shouted. "Don't hurt him! That's not Vester!"

Spud raised his voice. "That's what I keep telling this diminutive troglodyte."

Hildy almost laughed out loud. She would have to ask what those words meant. Right now, she was so happy she ran up to the older boy and started to reach out and grab his hands.

Then she stopped, embarrassed. "Hi," she said with a shy grin.

His answer surprised her. "Don't 'hi' me!" he snapped. "What kind of friends are you who'd run off and leave—?" His words broke off and he just stood there and stared. "You *are* a girl! Uh . . . you're *both* girls!"

For a moment, the importance of what Spud had said escaped Hildy. She turned to Cecil, who lowered his pitchfork uncertainly so the tines rested on the ground. Mr. Witt sat silently on his gelding a few feet away, his eyes taking in the situation.

Hildy quickly introduced the two men to the boy. Then she swung back to face Spud. "What do you mean: 'You *are* girls'? You didn't know *that* before."

Spud spoke softly to Lindy, and the dog relaxed his defensive stance and lay down on the boy's dusty shoes. "I ran into a Neanderthal hillbilly right after you and Tom . . . uh . . . whoever your obnoxious friend here is—"

Ruby walked up just in time to hear that remark. Raising her fists, she rushed at the boy. "What's that mean?"

Mr. Witt leaned down from the saddle and caught Ruby's arm as she charged by him. "Easy," he soothed in his soft, easy drawl. "Let's all go inside where we can get this whole thing straightened out."

Inside the kitchen, Spud was introduced to Mrs. Witt, and she invited everyone to sit down at the table. Spud put his aviator's cap on the back of his chair and smiled across the table at Hildy.

She felt funny. She wasn't sure if it was tension making knots in her stomach or her heart beating fast because Spud had shown up.

Spud sat forward. "I was so mad at you two for sneaking off on me in the Ozarks that I wanted to get even. Then I met a guy called Vester Hardesty."

Ruby jumped up from the table and started angrily around toward Spud. "Ye tol' Vester where we was a-goin'?"

Hildy grabbed Ruby and held her back.

"No," Spud protested. "I didn't. He wanted to know if I'd seen a couple of girls. I said no, but I'd walked awhile with two boys. That made Vester ask more questions. That's when I realized those 'boys' were really you two girls."

Spud looked down at his hands. "I also realized both of you had not only sneaked off without even a word, but you'd lied to me."

"We didn't do no sucha thing!" Ruby exploded.

"You misled me, anyway," Spud replied with some warmth. "You made me think you were boys. That's dishonest. Then you sneaked away and left me."

"I'm really sorry about that, Spud," Hildy apologized quietly.

The boy shrugged. "Well, anyway, this Vester told me that the woman who'd hired him to find you two said you'd either end up here or near Foleyville, Illinois. So Lindy and I headed here, figuring we could protect you from Vester, if you'd like, I mean."

Hildy was touched but didn't know what to say.

Mr. Witt cleared his throat. "Maybe that won't be necessary. My wife and I have come up with a solution to the girls' problem."

"What?" Hildy and Ruby exclaimed together.

Mr. Witt smiled. "You girls get washed up; then we'll all have breakfast, and I'll tell you."

CHAPTER
FIFTEEN

—

A CLUE TO THE PAST

As soon as the girls had washed up and brushed their hair, they all sat down and Mr. Witt said a prayer of thanks.

Then the rancher's wife began serving Spud some biscuits and country gravy. "I'm sure you girls won't mind if I start feeding this young man right away. No telling when he ate last."

Hildy shook her head pleasantly, but Ruby sat stonefaced.

Spud swallowed a bit of a hot biscuit and smiled across the table at Hildy.

Hildy nodded and returned the smile.

"I never saw you in a dress before," Spud remarked. The way he said it, Hildy felt sure he liked the way she looked.

"Mrs. Witt loaned it to me," she replied.

She saw his eyes rise to her hair, and her hands flew to her long unbraided brunette hair. "I had my hair in braids before, and we had to hide them under that cap so I'd look like a boy," she explained.

"That's a shame. You have pretty hair," Spud complimented her.

Flustered, Hildy quickly changed the subject. "Would you mind telling me how you ended up on the end of Uncle Cecil's pitchfork?"

Spud shrugged. "Well, I hitchhiked to Big Bend and found out where this ranch was; then I started walking and got here late last night. No lamps were burning. No dogs barked. So Lindy and I slept in the barn."

"And that's where Uncle Cecil found you?"

"Good thing you came along when you did," Spud said with a wry smile. "He wouldn't listen to my explanation at all."

Mr. Witt chuckled and held his coffee cup out to his wife for a refill. "May's well say this pronto, Hildy. You've got to call that place where your father works."

Hildy was disappointed. She had hoped Mr. Witt had a good plan for getting Ruby and her to Illinois. "That's what I've decided, too," she agreed, trying to sound cheerful.

"Good," the rancher replied. "Let's work out the details while we eat."

In twenty minutes, there was unanimous agreement around the table about what was to be done. Mr. Witt would drive Hildy and Ruby to the telephone in town. He would place the call and pay for it, and Hildy would talk to her father if he was there. If not, the rancher would talk to whomever answered.

Spud offered to go with Cecil to bring Blackie in, so Cecil gave him some jeans and boots he could wear in place of his knickers and floppy-soled shoes.

After breakfast while Hildy braided her hair again, the rancher's wife started gathering together some of her daughters' clothes for Hildy and Ruby to wear for the rest of the trip. There was no need to be in boys' disguise anymore.

Mr. Witt drove the girls into town in the noisy, chain-driven truck with hard rubber tires. They looked anxiously around for Vester but saw no sign of him. Stopping in front of the small corner drugstore, they went inside to use the town's only public phone. The druggist greeted them warmly, saying the lines were all back in service.

Hildy had never used a telephone before. In the right front corner of the store hung a square wooden box on the wall inside a small green metal booth. It had glass doors that opened in on themselves. The rancher explained a little about the instrument.

There was a small hand crank on the right-hand side of the box with a heavy black receiver upside down in a Y-shaped hook on the left. There were bells on top and a black mouthpiece stuck up about two inches from the box.

"It's about two hours earlier in California," Mr. Witt told the girls, "so we'll be lucky to catch your father. I'll call person-to-person. That way, if he's not there, it won't cost anything."

Hildy thought about how nice the old rancher was and swallowed hard. "I'll pay you back soon's I can," she said.

"I'm not doing anything for you two girls that I wouldn't do for my own daughters."

Hildy's eyes misted. A few days earlier she thought everybody in the world was mean and nasty. Then she met Spud, and Seth, and the Hightons, and Mr. and Mrs. Witt.

The rancher gave the phone crank a few brisk turns, then lifted the earpiece. "Hello, Central? I want to place a person-to-person call to Joe Corrigan at Lone River, California. The number is J-one-five-two. . . . Yes, I'll hold."

Hildy's heart thumped hard with excitement. Mr. Witt covered the mouthpiece with a calloused, deeply tanned hand and looked up at Hildy. "This is a farmer's line, so it's terribly noisy," he explained. "Got a bad hum. But if you shout a little and listen real close, you'll be able to hear him when he comes on the line."

Hildy nodded, barely able to speak. It seemed to take forever to make the connection. Finally the rancher moved his mouth closer to the phone.

"What, Operator? . . . He's not there?. . . . When do they expect him?" There was a pause and then, "He did?"

"What?" Hildy whispered. "What's happened?"

The rancher waved his free hand impatiently to quiet her so he could hear. "No," he said into the mouthpiece. "Just cancel the call."

Hildy swallowed hard, reading bad news in the rancher's eyes.

He hung up the receiver and gave the crank a brisk turn to clear the line. "Your father left for Illinois three days ago."

Disappointed but not surprised, Hildy nodded thoughtfully.

"At least we know the truth. I was afraid he was almost to Illinois already. We'll make it before he gets there."

Mr. Witt seemed doubtful. "It's only two days' drive if you can go straight through," he told her, "but so far, we don't have a way."

"There's got to be a way," Hildy said firmly. "Let's get back to the ranch so we can pack—"

"Hey!" Ruby interrupted. "Look out thar!"

Hildy's throat seemed to tighten and her heart jumped wildly. "Where?"

"Thar!" Ruby pointed through the drugstore window. "See that man by the truck?"

Hildy saw him then. His back was to the girls, but there was no doubt. It was Vester. "Oh, no!" Hildy groaned. "He's caught up with us!"

Hildy watched the heavyset man slowly walk by the Reo. Vester examined the truck carefully without stopping, then moved on down the street out of sight.

"What'll we do?" Ruby whispered in fear.

Mr. Witt put his arm around the girls protectively. "He won't try anything in town. Come on. Let's head for the ranch."

As they drove out of town, both girls checked behind them. Nobody was following.

Mr. Witt tightly gripped the truck's steering wheel. "This is more serious than I thought, girls. Tell you what—there's one way we can do this."

"What's that?" Hildy asked eagerly.

"I'll sell my horse and hire somebody to drive you to Illinois."

"Sell Blaze?" Ruby exclaimed.

He nodded, but Hildy shook her head violently. "Mr. Witt, we can't let you do that!"

"It's the only way left, Hildy, with the time limit you girls are facing and Vester hot on your trail."

"No, Mr. Witt," Hildy protested. "Thanks anyway, but you said yourself that's the best cow pony you ever owned."

"There's no other choice. This old truck won't stand another long trip without repairs, and Cecil's car certainly won't make it that far. That leaves only one alternative—selling Blaze."

"Oh, Mr. Witt!" Hildy cried, her voice breaking at the ranch-er's self-sacrificing offer. "There's got to be another way."

"Can you think of any?" he drawled.

"Well, no, not off hand, but—"

"Then let's say no more about it."

Hildy reluctantly obeyed, but she was heartsick. She and Ruby rode silently the rest of the way back to the ranch.

The rancher again parked the Reo in the barn as Cecil and Spud arrived with Blackie. Spud grinned broadly at Hildy. She didn't feel like smiling, but she did notice that he looked very good in his borrowed working-cowboy's outfit.

Spud took off a slightly worn-looking tan cowboy hat. "Blackie's fine," he said. "You'd never know she'd been hit by lightning except for the way her shoes were knocked clean off."

"Good," Mr. Witt said. "Come on inside everyone. We've got news and we've got a plan. See what you all think of it."

The rancher led the way toward the house just as dust rising from the main gravel road marked the progress of a car.

"That's Seth's car!" Hildy exclaimed, shading her eyes against the sun. "And he's got a passenger, so Rachel must be with him. Wonder why they're coming so early?" Everyone waited until the Model T chugged into the wide spot at the end of the driveway and stopped. Then they hurried over to greet the visitors.

Spud was introduced to Seth and Rachel while they still sat in the front seat. Then Seth looked at Rachel and asked, "Ye want to tell 'em, honey?"

She lowered her eyes. "You do it," she murmured.

The mountaineer turned and grinned broadly, looking quickly to the others gathered around outside the car. "My ma wanted Rachel and me to git married at Ol' Bethel at home, but . . . well . . ." His voice trailed off.

"You're married?" Hildy cried joyously.

"This mornin'," Seth announced proudly. "We drove inta town and Rachel's pastor married us not more'n an hour ago."

There were glad cries of congratulation all around, and Mrs.

Witt came hurrying out of the house just in time to join in. She urged everyone to come inside.

"Much obliged, Miz Witt," Seth replied, "but . . . well, I saved me some money jist in case Rachel said yes, so we're startin' our honeymoon right now!"

"To Chicago," Rachel added with a shy smile.

Seth paused dramatically, then continued slowly. "Since it's right on our way, we'd like to take Hildy and Ruby along an' drop 'em off at Foleyville."

Tears of surprise and joy sprang to Hildy's eyes, and a big lump formed in her throat. She couldn't speak.

"On your honeymoon?" Mrs. Witt asked.

Seth lowered his eyes and nodded. "Rachel an' me done decided."

Rachel reached out to the girls through the window. "Please get ready, girls," she said softly.

Things happened too fast for Hildy to remember.

In an hour, Hildy and Ruby stood by the Model T Ford in borrowed dresses and shoes. Their tow sacks had been replaced by an old wicker suitcase that the Witts insisted they didn't want anymore.

Hildy hated goodbyes. She wanted them over as quickly as possible, but she started with Mr. Witt. He surprised Hildy by giving her a bone-crushing hug.

Mrs. Witt pulled Hildy and Ruby together into her motherly arms. When she released them, the rancher's wife looked tenderly at Ruby.

"I don't know if this will interest you," Mrs. Witt began, extending an old sepia-tone photograph. "I found it with several old pictures when I emptied that suitcase we gave you girls."

Hildy peeked over Ruby's shoulder as her cousin looked at a snapshot of a handsome, smiling man on horseback. Wearing a tall western hat, denim jacket, leather chaps, and cowboy boots, he sat straight and tall in the saddle, his hands resting on the horn.

Ruby frowned, not understanding.

Mrs. Witt continued. "The moment I saw the picture, it all

came back to me. We called him Highpockets because he was so tall. I don't remember his real first name, but his last name was the same as yours, Ruby—Konning. Spelled with a *K*."

Hildy's mouth dropped open in surprise.

Ruby looked up at Mrs. Witt. "Ye mean . . . this here's a pi'ture of . . . my daddy?" she asked softly.

"I don't know, dear," Mrs. Witt replied, placing a gentle hand on the girl's shoulder. "He came here shortly after the war—about twelve or thirteen years ago, I guess. Maybe stayed a year, then drifted on. That's why neither my husband nor I could remember him when we heard your surname. But it's written on the back."

Ruby turned the photograph over.

Hildy leaned forward and read the ink handwriting: "Highpockets Konning, 1921."

Ruby's eyes were filled with wonder and hope. "Whar'd he go when he left here?" she asked breathlessly.

"It's been so long ago, but seems to me it was somewhere in California."

Mr. Witt moved closer to examine the photo. "Say, I remember him now. Good ranch hand, but not very talkative. Never said much about himself."

"Please," Ruby begged. "Cain't ye 'member whar egzackly he was a-goin'?"

The Witts looked at each other and shook their heads.

Then Mr. Witt snapped his fingers. "Hey, wait! It was Grizzly Gulch! I remember because it's a funny name! He said to forward any mail to him there in care of general delivery, but I don't remember if he ever got any."

Ruby reached out, impulsively hugging the rancher and his wife together. They held her close for a moment. When Ruby stepped back, still gripping the photograph, her eyes were filled with tears—and hope.

Seth cleared his throat. "I'm right sorry to break this up, but we's got to be a-goin'."

"Jist one more question," Ruby said. She looked hopefully at the Witts. "Did . . . did he ever mention havin' ary daughter?"

The rancher and his wife exchanged glances.

"Like I said," Mr. Witt drawled, "he didn't talk much. But please keep the picture, Ruby."

"Thankee kindly," Ruby whispered.

Mrs. Witt hugged the girls and murmured, "Ruby, I hope you find your father someday. God bless you both. You'll be in our prayers."

Ruby looked like she was about to cry. She only nodded.

Hildy turned to Cecil and gave him a kiss on the cheek. "Thanks for everything! I'm glad you're my uncle."

"Good luck to you both," the wiry little cowboy answered.

As Hildy and Ruby turned to face Spud, Ruby nodded, saying briefly, "See ye."

The boy nodded in return, but his eyes were on Hildy.

Not knowing what to say, she blurted the first thing that came into her mind. "Someday I hope you come to California and teach me more about words. You know, like *curmudgeon* and *troglodyte*?"

Spud's eyes widened in surprise. "You know what those words mean?"

"No, but soon's I can, I'll get a dictionary and look them up."

Spud reached into his back pocket and whipped out his frayed and battered dictionary. "Here," he offered, thrusting it into her hands.

"Oh, I can't—"

"You can give it back when I see you again," Spud replied quietly. "Until then—"

"Hildy, Ruby," Seth interrupted. "We's got to be a-movin'."

A few minutes later, the Model T and its four passengers pulled onto the main road from the ranch. A quarter mile behind them, another car eased away from the roadside and followed the Ford.

CHAPTER
SIXTEEN

———

A SCREAM IN THE NIGHT

Seth turned around in the front seat of the old Model T Ford. "Gals, me'n Rachel done talked it over. We figger to drive purty much straight through. Don't want y'all to miss yore daddy. If'n I git sleepy, we'll pull off'n the road and rest a spell, then go on."

Rachel smiled at the two girls. "Don't neither of you fret. Unless this ol' car breaks down, we'll make it to Foleyville in plenty of time."

Hildy felt a vague uneasiness. "Break down?" she asked, leaning forward a little.

Seth laughed. "We ain't 'spectin' no trouble, Hildy. But this here Model T is purty old for such long, hard runnin'. Still, I kin fix most anythin' that goes wrong with it, so even if'n it does, shouldn't be long afore we're rollin' agin. Don't worry none."

Hildy relaxed. "How'd you two meet?" she asked.

That started a long conversation, with Seth and his bride taking turns, remembering how they had met years before, broke up, and then got back together again. They spoke excitedly of their plans to return to the Ozarks and make their home there.

"But we's both always wanted to see Chicago," Seth concluded, "so we're a-headin' thar, then back to the Ozarks."

From the backseat, Hildy and Ruby shared their experiences at the ranch. When Ruby told about Blackie being hit by lightning while her cousin sat on the mare's back, Hildy again shuddered to think of how close she had come to being killed.

She did not tell about her short prayer the night before or how she had felt afterward. It was too soon to talk about that. Yet somehow Hildy felt something had happened. It was like turning a corner.

Slowly, as the morning ended, conversation lagged. Hildy began thinking about seeing Molly and the kids, wondering what to say to her stepmother. *What if Molly refuses to let me back into the family?* she thought. *What would Daddy say?*

Hildy shook her head. *This is between Molly and me*, she told herself. *I've got to talk to her and work things out before Daddy gets there. The main thing is to keep the family together!*

Ruby slouched on the black seat cushion beside Hildy and looked at the photograph Mrs. Witt had given her. "Ye reckon this here's really my pa?" she asked Hildy quietly.

"There's no way of knowing, but maybe."

"Wouldn't it be somethin' if'n I found him out in Californy after all these years? Then someday he'n me'd go back home to all them people who said hurtful things 'bout me. I'd show 'em! I'd say, 'This here's my daddy that my mother used to tell ye 'bout and ye wouldn't believe her.' "

Hildy reached over and gave Ruby a couple of quick pats on her forearm. Hildy ached for her cousin and all those years of painful memories. She understood Ruby's wishful thinking, yet didn't dare risk raising her cousin's hopes.

Shifting to make herself more comfortable, she looked through the small window in the back of the Model T. Dust rose in the distance, marking the progress of another car behind them.

For a second, Hildy thought it might be Vester. She shook her head. *He's got no car*, she told herself firmly. *And he's got no money to buy one, either. Granny wouldn't give him that much*. Hildy took her eyes off the dust cloud and refused to look back again.

Some time well after the sun had peaked in the sky and started down, Rachel opened two shiny old tin pails with light bails or handles. The tins had once held lard and molasses. Hildy had often seen similar containers at school. Many of the kids brought their lunches in them. Rachel took sandwiches from the pails and handed them out. Everyone ate while Seth drove on. Seth managed to eat his sandwich with one hand as he held the steering wheel with the other.

After they were finished eating, Hildy produced Spud's dictionary and looked up the word *curmudgeon*. "A surly, churlish person," said the dictionary. Then Hildy found the word *troglodyte*. "Cave dweller," it said. Hildy smiled. That didn't exactly fit Uncle Cecil. Still, maybe Spud thought the small cowboy looked like a caveman when he threatened Spud with the pitchfork.

Some time later, Seth stopped on a desolate stretch of road. He got out of the car and took the canvas water bag from the left front bumper where it was kept cool by the wind passing over it. Removing the cork stopper, he passed the bag around and everyone took a drink.

Hildy didn't think anything of it. At school, everyone drank from the same water bucket and long-handled dipper.

Hildy walked around the car a few times to stretch her legs. After the bouncing, jerking ride and the noise of the motor, the silence was welcome. The only noise they could hear was the wind sighing through the tall grass at the side of the road.

As Hildy gazed out over the endless, rolling prairie, she felt a terrible loneliness. Even the road behind them was empty and silent. There was no gravel on this stretch. It was only dirt and dust. There was no plume of dust in the distance, so Hildy sighed with relief. If there had been a car following them, it had turned off.

Or stopped. The thought terrified Hildy, and she could hardly wait to get started again.

A minute after Seth eased the flivver onto the rutted road, Hildy looked back.

A rooster's tail of dust again rose in the distance. *Couldn't be Vester*, she tried to tell herself, *. . . unless . . . he stole a car.*

Hildy swallowed hard, shivering with all her old fears. She tried to control her thoughts. *Naw, Vester probably doesn't even know how to drive anything but a team of horses or mules. Can't be him.*

She didn't mention the trailing car to the others. If Seth was driving steadily as fast as the rutted road would allow, they would reach Foleyville safely—as long as the Model T kept moving.

The sun was sinking fast, painting the clouds with beautiful shades of pink and orange. Everyone but Seth had dozed, and there had been no conversation in the car for a long time. Ruby was asleep, so Hildy shifted position and let her mind wander.

I wonder what Spud's real name is? she thought. Reaching down to the corner where she had placed Spud's dictionary, she put the battered book on her lap and opened it. There in front, neatly scripted words in blue ink proclaimed: "Stolen from Conlan Carlin Lawler."

Hildy smiled and impulsively clutched the book close to her chest. *That has to be his name*, she thought. *Anybody else would have written, "This book belongs to . . ."*

She glanced down again at the page and saw something else written faintly in pencil. "Conlan: Irish Gaelic; mumbler, half-speaker. Carlin: Old Gaelic Irish, Little Champion. Lawler: Irish Gaelic, Hero."

He even looked up what his name means! she thought. *Hmm? I wonder if they called him Conlan or Carlin at home? What nice names! Irish champion and hero! But he didn't like it somehow; otherwise, why would he call himself Spud?*

As darkness fell, Seth stopped for gasoline in a small town. Rachel treated the girls to ice cold Nehi strawberry sodas while she picked up some "fixin's" for supper. When they started driving again, Seth turned on the car's headlights.

Hildy swiveled in the backseat to look out the rear window.

Far behind, a pair of headlights winked on. There was no longer any doubt in the girl's mind. *Vester is following us!* she concluded. *He must be waiting for an opportunity to get Ruby and me alone. Well, we won't let that happen.*

Knowing that their pursuer was biding his time in following, Hildy was glad that Seth continued to drive steadily into the night.

"Highpockets." Ruby barely spoke the word aloud from the darkness.

"What?" Hildy asked.

"Huh? Oh, I been a-thinkin' 'bout that thar pi'ture Miz Witt give me."

Hildy stared ahead as the Ford's headlights bounced hard on what Seth had called a "washboard road."

Ruby continued. "My mama tol' me that pa's Christian name was Nathaniel. But she called him Nate. Nate Konning. That's what she tol' me. Ye reckon he's still at Grizzly Gulch? Hmm?"

"It's been thirteen years, Ruby. And . . . that may not be him."

"I know, but I kin hope. I wonder if Grizzly Gulch is on a Californy map? Mebby I kin git one and see."

Hildy didn't reply. Her mind leaped back to their silent pursuer. Should she say anything to the others?

She decided to wait. Ruby didn't say anything more, and soon Hildy dozed off. She slept fitfully, dreaming of Vester sneaking up and snatching her. She screamed, but it was silent. Hildy dreamed she was carried off like a tow sack of potatoes into the distance.

She awoke with a start and sat up, heart pounding. *Only a dream!* She took a deep breath, then realized that the Ford was parked on the side of the road with its headlights off. The car was in total darkness. Only a thin, bacon rind of a moon shone. Hildy could barely make out a bulky shadow in the front seat. She thought Seth and Rachel were sitting up very close together because they seemed to be only one person.

Hildy turned to look out the back window, but the moonlight was so weak that there was only a sense of the vast, empty land around them. Yet there was something else—a kind of darker bulk, like a boxy sedan against the skyline. Hildy stared until tiny flecks of light danced in front of her eyes.

Is it a car? she wondered.

A second later she caught a tiny wink of light. It was as though the moonlight had reflected off something—possibly the hood ornament.

Fear seized Hildy. *It's Vester! He's parked beside the road, too. Watching us! Must've shifted his weight or something so the car moved and the moonbeams hit something shiny.*

Then another thought struck. *Or maybe he was getting out of the car to try sneaking up on us!*

She sat still, so tense she would have twanged like a mandolin string if somebody had touched her. All her senses were alert, especially her eyes and ears.

Through the open side of the car Hildy heard a sound. She leaned forward, barely breathing, trying to peer through the darkness that surrounded the Ford.

A faint footstep. Hildy's heart started beating faster. Another. Coming straight toward the car, but so quietly that Hildy had to strain hard to hear at all.

Swallowing hard, she tried to decide what to do. She started to lean forward to touch Seth on the shoulder, then stopped in terror. Out of the corner of her eye, she saw a man's silhouette move silently out of the moonlight to the running board. His arm reached out toward the car.

"No!" Hildy screamed, lashing out with both hands. "Seth! Seth! Wake up!"

The man jerked his hand back from the car. "Shhh!" he commanded.

Hildy threw herself backward across the seat against Ruby.

The dark shadow on the front seat seemed to erupt.

So did Ruby. "Why're ye screechin' loud 'nuff to wake up a deef man?" she demanded, shoving angrily against Hildy.

Rachel's anxious voice came from the front seat. "Are you all right, Hildy?"

"Where's Seth?" Hildy nearly screeched.

"I'm rahtchere, aside ye, jist outside the car."

Hildy's heart was beating so fast it took her a moment to be sure. Slowly, she made out the mountaineer's head and shoulders. "Seth?" she whispered.

"Nobody else but." He slid behind the wheel. "I got tahrd of that thar feller afollerin' us like an old redbone houn' on a hot trail. So I done slowed him up a mite."

"You knew he was following?"

"From the time we'uns turned out of the Witts' place," Seth said.

Hildy started to tell them that she didn't say anything because she didn't want to worry them, but she stopped at a now-familiar sound. The ignition buzzed.

Seth continued. "So I jist parked an' waited until I figgered that Vester feller was asleep. Then I snuck back like a Injun an' let the air out of one tahr."

The mountaineer laughed softly and straightened up. "I took the valve stem outta his spare tahr on the back end, too. Slow him up even more, a-fixin' both them tahrs. Well, we best get movin' 'case he heard yore scream." He climbed back out and walked around to the front of the Ford.

Rachel turned in the front seat and spoke into the darkness. "Ain't Seth the cat's meow, girls?"

"Sure is," Hildy agreed.

The engine began to turn over, then caught. As Seth choked it, the car started to creep forward.

Ruby rubbed her eyes and muttered, "Would y'all tell me what's a-goin' on?"

"In a minute," Hildy replied.

Climbing behind the wheel again, Seth switched on the headlights and eased the Model T back onto the rutted road.

Hildy turned to look back. Headlights came on, but the car behind them didn't pull onto the road. Hildy saw a man's shadow pass in front of the lights. A moment later, she saw the silhouette of a leg kicking at the car.

From the Ford's front seat, Seth began singing happily, "If I had the wings of an angel. . . ."

Hildy leaned back and smiled. "Now I'll tell you, Ruby," she said.

Ruby frowned. "First, let me tell ye somethin'!" she growled. "If'n ye ever let out a squawl in my ear like ye jist done, y'all never git to Illinois! Yore screechin' like to of made me deef."

Hildy laughed. "I won't do it again. I promise."

As the car bounced on through the night, its passengers slipped away from one danger and headed straight toward another.

CHAPTER Seventeen

TORNADO!

They were more than twenty-four hours out of Big Bend when Hildy awoke from where she had dozed in the backseat with Ruby. Rachel's head lay against her new husband's shoulder.

Hildy leaned forward to touch the front seat behind the driver. "Where are we?" she asked above the shaking, rattling noise of the car.

"Don't rightly know," Seth replied. "More'n halfway, I reckon. But this here washboard road is comin' near to shakin' us to pieces. Worst stretch yet."

The Model T was the only thing moving across a barren, desolate land. There were no buildings except an occasional farmhouse in the distance.

The afternoon air was hot and still. Even the warm breeze generated by the Ford's steady movement didn't lessen Hildy's discomfort. She fanned herself with Spud's dictionary, but that didn't help, either.

Seth drove mechanically through the stifling heat. The car bounced and pitched on the mostly rutted dirt road with some stretches of gravel. No one maintained this road, so it was all very rough.

Hildy couldn't believe how alert Seth seemed after having driven steadily until some time after midnight. Then he pulled off the road and slept awhile. His dollar pocket watch had stopped, he'd explained, and so he didn't know how long they had actually been driving.

He turned his head. "Nobody's a-follerin' us," he remarked with a smile.

Hildy looked out the back window. There wasn't a thing moving anywhere except the Ford.

As she glanced at the sky, the sun disappeared behind a dark cloud. *Another thunderstorm coming up*, she thought. It made her a little nervous, remembering her frightening experience with Blackie.

Ruby opened her eyes. "I done drempt I found my pa," she said softly.

Hildy could tell by the tone of her cousin's voice that she was sorry it was only a dream.

Rachel stirred from the front seat and turned around. "People need dreams, Ruby."

Ruby pursed her lips thoughtfully. "'Specially if life kicks ye in the teeth from the secont yore borned."

The bride twisted still farther around in the front seat, and Ruby leaned forward so they could talk better above the jostling and noise of the old car.

Rachel smiled at Ruby. "Where ye come from may not be your choice, but where ye go *is* your choice," she said.

"Dunno's I agree with ye on that," Ruby muttered.

"I had a wise ol' grandmother," Rachel continued. "She'd never been out of the Ozarks, probably never more'n a few miles from where she was born. But she used to say, 'Rachel, ye kin overcome the past and change yore future by the choices ye make from now on.'"

Ruby nodded soberly. "Well, I never had no choict in the way I got started in life—that's fer shore."

Hildy listened quietly. Out of habit, she still occasionally turned her head to peer out the small rear window. Throughout the morning, she had from time to time seen wagons and a couple of buggies. But they would soon be left in the distance. Once an Indian motorcycle with a sidecar had followed them awhile but it turned off into a farmer's lane.

Not once had there been the steady plume of dust that had marked Vester's trailing them the first day. There was no one behind them now in the waning afternoon, and Hildy sighed with relief.

"Rachel," Ruby mused, "how d'ye know when yore makin' the right choict?"

The new bride smiled comfortingly. "My grandmother had a saying for that, too. She'd say, 'God can help ye make the right choices and redirect yore future.' That's what she'd say."

Hildy saw a shadow pass over the car. She leaned sideways and looked out at the sky. "Storm's coming on fast," she said.

Seth lowered his head and looked all around the horizon. "Yore right. It could blow in on us and soak ever'body. Reckon I better stop and put up the side curtains."

Hildy was afraid to say anything, but she wanted to keep going. She knew that Vester had only been delayed; he would not quit. He was probably really mad now because he had fallen asleep, allowing Seth to let the air out of his tires.

Hildy wouldn't feel safe until she was with her father. He would send Vester packing so fast that the varmint wouldn't slow down till he got back to the Ozarks. *And Granny would eat him alive*, Hildy thought with a smile. *It'd serve him right.*

Rachel turned to her new husband. "Can we help ye with the side curtains, dear?"

Seth eased the Ford off the road. "Mebby in a little bit. Got to git them out first."

As Hildy and Ruby started to get out of the backseat, Rachel spoke again, and both girls sat back down. "Ruby, I hope ye won't mind me saying this, but . . . well . . . I feel like we're getting to be pretty good friends, so—"

"We're friends," Ruby agreed.

"Well, sometimes life gives us a bad start through no fault of our own," Rachel said. "But the unfortunate circumstances of your birth can only keep on hurting your life if ye let them."

Hildy thought that made sense. "Now you've got some hope of finding your father, Ruby," she added. "But even if you don't find him, you can at least live peaceably with all that's happened to you."

"That's true, Ruby," Rachel told her. "Why, maybe he doesn't even know ye were ever born, so he'd have no reason to hunt for ye."

"I thought on that," Ruby answered.

Thunder rumbled in the distance and Hildy looked up quickly as the countryside lit up with steady flashes of lightning. The sky was getting black fast—faster than Hildy could ever remember. She glanced down from the threatening storm to Rachel's and Ruby's faces. They also seemed to sense danger.

Seth was standing on the ground by the driver's side when he took a sudden, sharp breath. "Look!" he cried, jabbing his bare forearm out straight. "Look!"

At first Hildy saw only dark clouds about two miles away, moving very fast on powerful winds. "What?" she asked, straining to see what had excited the mountaineer. "I don't see—"

Then she saw it!

A whirling, funnel-shaped cloud lowered itself from the dark, shifting, churning mass.

Hildy sucked in her breath. "Tornado!"

She had studied these dangerous storms in her one-room school. She had also heard of tornados that struck near her home. Now one of the most destructive forces in nature was forming in front of her eyes and coming straight for them.

Suddenly the wind struck the Ford, rocking it back and forth.

"Oh, Seth!" Rachel cried anxiously. "What do we do?"

Seth desperately looked around for a place of safety.

In school Rachel had learned that a cellar was best, but there wasn't even a farmhouse in sight.

Hildy focused her attention on the dark terror sweeping toward them. Numbed by panic, she watched as the funnel-shaped cloud finished its descent from the parent cloud overhead. Dark and flexible, it twisted and writhed like an elephant's trunk.

Ruby grabbed Hildy's arm. "Look! Thar's another one! An' another!"

Hildy's blue eyes flashed upward. It was true! To the left of the original funnel-shaped cloud, another broke off from the dark mass overhead and stretched its narrow trunk to the ground. At almost the same instant, a third funnel formed to the right of the original.

"They're joinin' up!" Ruby yelled. "All three done mixed inta one! An' it's a-headin' right fer us!"

Seth stuck his head inside the car and turned on the ignition. "I'll crank 'er up and head fer a holler I see over thar."

Hildy was so scared she could barely move as the twister swept toward them in a quarter-mile-wide front. Bits of debris swirled violently up into the sky and then scattered wildly outside the black, twisting monster.

"Oh, Lord!" Hildy heard herself praying. "Oh, Lord, help!" Grabbing for the sides of the car, she hung on as the Ford bounced crazily off the road and plunged like a frightened animal into a small, shallow ditch. The car shuddered to a stop just as a thick blackness and shrieking wind engulfed them.

Seth was shouting something, but Hildy couldn't make out the words. He grabbed Rachel and dove onto the front floorboards crowded with handles and pedals.

Hildy wanted to jump out and run, but there was no time. The loudest noise she had ever heard tore at her ears. She and Ruby crouched on the floor between the seats, instinctively holding their hands over their heads for protection.

The Ford teetered and rocked, threatening to blow over. Once it almost lifted entirely off the ground. Hildy heard the canvas top rip off.

She didn't know how long the incredible roaring lasted, but finally it was over. For a moment, she was afraid to believe it. Fearfully, she raised her head.

Seth peeked over the backseat. "Ever'body okay?"

Slowly, the other three heads rose above the seat level. The car roof was gone except for some tattered pieces. All four of them instinctively reached out and hugged each other across the front seat.

Seth looked around in awe. "It musta barely brushed us, or we'uns wouldn't still be here!" he whispered.

Hildy took a slow, shuddering breath of relief. Ruby's eyes were wide with fright as though she couldn't believe they were still alive.

Rachel's face looked pale. "Let's say thanks," she suggested.

Hildy lowered her head and closed her eyes. "Thanks, Lord!" She had definitely turned a corner. When she opened her eyes, she noticed that Ruby had not bowed her head. The anger and pain of years was still too great. Pulling the photograph from her dress pocket, Ruby looked at it longingly. Her eyes softened.

Seth cranked the car again and hopped behind the steering wheel. "Well, let's git on down the road."

"Yes," Hildy whispered, "and let's hope nothing else happens until we get to Molly's parents' house!"

Early the next morning, under a beautiful sunny sky, they crossed the Mississippi River from St. Louis into Illinois.

Hildy leaned forward eagerly as the Model T eventually passed from the sandy road onto a cobblestone street at the edge of Foleyville. It was a railroad town, smelling of creosote and coal smoke.

Memories stirred within Hildy. She glanced excitedly around and announced, "My granddad Corrigan used to sell hardwood trees from his farm for railroad ties, so he'd bring me here, riding on the ties on his sledge.

"His farm's on the other side of town, so we'd hitch up the team and pull the loaded sledge past the town clock in the bank tower. See it 'way off in the distance?"

"I see it," Ruby answered.

Hildy added, "We'd take the ties over there to the right, where all those railroad spur tracks with old boxcars and gondolas are standing."

"Ye mean beyond that buildin' jist ahead an' to the right?" Ruby asked.

"Yes. That's the depot. You see the set of railroad tracks

running just in back of it? That's for passengers who get on or off the train there."

"Shore air a powerful lot of other tracks beyond that thar one," Ruby remarked with awe.

"Those are the railroad yards," Hildy explained, pointing. "Look, 'way in back there? Well, just beyond the middle of the yards is the main line for freight trains. Actually, there're two lines side-by-side."

Seth asked, "Y'all a-sayin' three trains could go through here at one time?"

"Granddad said so! One freight train could be going north toward Chicago on one of those far tracks while another freight would be going south. They'd meet and pass each other a few feet apart. Now, up closer, see by the depot, there could be a third train."

"A passenger train?" Seth asked.

"Yes. The passenger train could be going either way, because just outside of town a couple miles, the tracks turn so people can ride either east or west."

Ruby, the Ozark-reared girl, stared open-mouthed at the maze of tracks and sidings as the Model T rattled along the cobblestone street.

Hildy said, "We're passing the depot now. This street turns to the right up ahead and heads into downtown. The business section is just beyond the freight yards."

"Shore is a powerful sight to see!" Ruby murmured. She turned to Hildy. "Ye reckon maybe we'uns kin ride one of them trains someday?"

"Maybe," Hildy replied.

Seth pulled into a gas station to ask directions to the Holloway farm.

As the Ford bounced along the final miles of flat land toward Molly's parents' place, Hildy was so excited she could hardly breathe.

Farmers with teams of mules or horses waved as the Ford passed. Seth pointed out something none of them had ever seen before: a tractor dragging a plow across the fields.

As Seth turned off the main graveled road onto a long, narrow dirt lane, Hildy took one last, reassuring look behind. Nobody was following.

"We made it," she whispered. "We made it!"

Now she faced the problem of dealing with Molly about what had happened a few days earlier.

Everyone in the car fell silent as the roofless touring car crept along through tall brush that touched the high, black fenders on both sides of the car. The lane twisted to the right, and Hildy saw tall maple trees and an open gate to a dusty driveway. Raising her eyes, she caught sight of the farmhouse tucked away among the big trees.

It was a solid, two-story white structure in need of paint. The Depression prevented most people from doing simple house maintenance. Behind the farmhouse stood a smokehouse, harness shed, barn, outhouse, and silo.

Hildy's emotions fought within her. *What'll Molly do when she sees me? Run me off like a stray cat or let me talk? What has she told the kids about me not being with them? What if she's turned them against me? What's she told my father? What if she doesn't want me back?*

Ruby's voice broke into Hildy's thoughts. "Whar's the kids?" she asked. "They should be outside a-playin' on this kind of purty day."

Where were her sisters and brother? Hildy's eager blue eyes hurriedly swept the area but saw no children. She did not hear them, either. There was only a terrible, threatening silence.

"Maybe they's already gone on to Californy," Ruby whispered.

Seth eased the Ford under the shade of a wide-spreading maple and turned off the motor. "Hildy, ye want us to go in with ye?" he asked, looking over his shoulder.

She shook her head and opened the back door. "No," she said, stepping on the running board and then the ground. "Please wait here a minute until I find out what Molly's going to do when she sees me."

Shakily, she walked to the high wooden porch and climbed

the stairs, which seemed to boom loudly with each step. *No dogs barking*, she thought. Taking a deep breath, she knocked at the door. *Maybe nobody's home.*

She listened. There was no sound inside the house. With growing concern, Hildy knocked again. *What if Ruby was right? What if Dad had arrived early and taken the family back to California?*

Ruby called to her in a loud whisper. "Behind the house! Somebody's a-comin'!"

Hildy walked to the edge of the porch and peered around the end of the house. A woman in her middle thirties walked under the trees beside the house. Wearing a wide-brimmed hat and an old dress, she held a sagging, heavily loaded apron away from her body.

"Molly," Hildy murmured, her throat suddenly dry. "It's me."

The woman stopped stock-still. Her mouth dropped open and both hands flew to it. The eggs she had been carrying in her apron smashed in a mess all over her shoes.

Hildy's stepmother didn't seem to notice. She just stood there, saying nothing.

"Molly," Hildy murmured again, louder. "It's me, Hildy."

The woman still did not move, apparently unable to believe what she saw. Her brown eyes were wide as saucers. A flush swept over Molly's cheeks, and her fingers rested against her mouth, trembling.

Hildy had never seen such a look on anyone's face, and it scared her. Her worst fears seemed confirmed. Molly didn't want her and never expected to see her again.

Slowly, with a terribly sick feeling, the girl turned and walked woodenly across the porch and down the stairs. In total dejection, head down, Hildy headed for the car.

Then she heard a sharp intake of breath behind her. "It's Hildy! Oh, my Lord, it *is* her!"

The girl turned to see Molly start running straight toward her, broken egg yolks flying from her shoes.

Frightened, Hildy rushed blindly back to the car.

In all Hildy's imaginings about what might happen when she next met her stepmother, Hildy had never expected to be attacked by her.

CHAPTER EIGHTEEN

KIDNAPPED!

Hildy sprinted toward the car with Molly right behind her, gaining fast. Suddenly her stepmother grasped Hildy's left arm and spun her around. Molly wasn't much taller than Hildy, but she was very strong. Hildy struggled to jerk loose, but Molly instantly grabbed the girl's other wrist and clamped down hard.

Molly's brown eyes bore into Hildy's blue ones. The color had gone from Molly's cheeks. Her mouth hung half open, working soundlessly.

Hildy desperately tried to pull away, but Molly clasped both her arms tightly around the girl's thin shoulders. Hildy had never felt such strength in a woman. "Molly, please!" she cried. "I'll leave, just tell me where the kids are."

Molly moaned. "Oh, Hildy! Hildy! Forgive me!" She looked up into the sky. "Oh, God, please forgive me."

Hildy couldn't believe what she was hearing. Jerking her head back from Molly's, she saw her stepmother's eyes wet with tears and her face twisted in pain.

"Oh, Hildy!" she cried hoarsely. "Please say you forgive me."

Hildy studied the anguished face so close to hers. Unable to speak, Hildy clutched her stepmother closer to her and broke into big sobs.

The two were still hugging each other when Seth, Rachel, and Ruby quietly walked up. Seth cleared his throat, and Hildy managed to control her emotions long enough to introduce the newlyweds to her stepmother.

Molly shook hands with Seth and Rachel, then hugged Ruby.

Surprised, Ruby hung back stiffly in Molly's arms. Nobody ever hugged Ruby. But slowly the girl's arms relaxed. She reached up and returned the woman's hug.

Seth shifted from one foot to the other and began to explain how they all came to be there. "Rachel and me was a-headin' this way, so we give these two gals a ride," he concluded. "But now, if'n it's okay by ever'body, we'll be gittin' along down the road."

"What?" Molly cried, sniffing and wiping her eyes with the back of her hands. "Excuse my manners. Everybody come inside and rest a spell."

She glanced at her shoes. "Oh, look at that. I'll never get those eggs off." She reached down, pulled the shoes off and stood in stocking feet. "Anyway, come in. Come in."

Hildy laughed, more from relief than anything else. She swung in beside her stepmother. Like her brother, Molly wasn't very tall.

"Where're my sisters and baby brother?" Hildy asked.

"They're in town with my parents," Molly replied. "They'll be back soon. Oh, will they be surprised and happy to see you, Hildy!"

"I can hardly wait to see them! Have you heard from Daddy?"

"I talked to him long distance a few days ago. He's on his way here. Could arrive today or tomorrow. Then we're all going to California to live. Won't that be wonderful?"

"Wonderful!" Hildy agreed happily. As an afterthought, she asked, "Does he know about me . . . uh . . . staying behind in the Ozarks?"

"I was going to tell him when he got here. It's too hard to explain long distance."

"Then don't say anything," Hildy urged.

"Oh, Hildy!" Molly reached out quickly and put her arm around Hildy's shoulders. The two hurried through the screened-in back porch.

In a few minutes, they all sat in the parlor, which smelled of dust and age. It obviously hadn't been used often. Ornate oval frames hung from wires on the wall. The stern-faced people peering from the old photographs were Molly and Cecil's ancestors, she told them.

Molly brought out a plate of cookies and some glasses of milk, then sat down and looked at her stepdaughter with eyes still bright from tears. "Hildy, I realized after it was too late how wrong I was. I should never have left you behind without a word, even though your grandmother convinced me that's what you wanted."

Seth stood up. "Er . . . maybe you two should be alone."

"No, please." Molly reached out to him. Her light brown hair had a few streaks of gray that Hildy had never noticed before. Molly's face was pretty, the girl decided—not as pretty as Hildy's mother had been, but Molly was a nice-looking woman. No doubt about that. Hildy could understand why her father had been attracted to Molly.

"Well," Seth said uncertainly, helping himself to a cookie, "if'n yore shore?"

"I'm positive," Molly assured him. "I want all of you to hear this."

Seth sat back down by Rachel. Ruby remained unusually quiet, sitting in a big overstuffed chair and sipping a cold glass of milk.

Molly turned to Hildy and took her hand. "I thought you resented me for coming into the family so soon after your mother's death."

Hildy didn't say anything. She remembered how she had felt. Her stepmother was right.

Molly continued. "Marriage isn't something stepchildren understand too well. Joe was lonesome, and so was I. My husband had been dead a long time. Our only child had died two years before. Joe needed someone to help with all his kids. And, after all, he and I had known each other a long time."

Hildy silently struggled with her own thoughts. She had forgotten how much she had resented her new stepmother at first. *And I was sure Daddy didn't think I did a good enough job with the younger kids*, she reminded herself. But for the past few days, all Hildy could think of was that Molly had left with the kids, leaving Hildy behind.

Molly leaned forward and looked deep into Hildy's eyes. "Oh, I know you were doing a great job as a substitute mother, Hildy. For a twelve-year-old, you couldn't be beat! But Joe needed a grown woman, so when he asked me, I married him."

Hildy fidgeted nervously and started to speak.

"No, please. Don't say anything yet, Hildy. Let me finish. You see, I thought that in time you'd understand. But it wasn't long after Joe and I were married before I began to feel you resented me. It was worse because your father had to leave us so soon to go looking for work. Then when he found a job in California and decided he had made enough to bring us all out there, I told your grandmother."

She shook her head slowly. "You weren't home that day. You were with Ruby. I made a mistake. I told your granny instead of saying anything to you."

Molly's eyes clouded with remembered pain. Her voice was low and weak. "Your grandmother told me that you hated me and wished you didn't have to live under the same roof with me."

Hildy jumped up. "I never said any such a thing!"

Molly nodded, her lower lip trembling. "I should have known that. I should have! But I was so hurt that you didn't like me when I was trying so hard to love all of you, to make a home for you kids while your father was away. But I should have checked with you first—" Her sentence dissolved into painful sobs.

Hildy reached out and tenderly touched her stepmother's shoulder. "I'm sorry, Molly. I shouldn't have doubted you," she said, beginning to cry.

Molly held out her arms and Hildy slid into them. Holding

each other close, they softly murmured reassurances through
their tears.

Seth stood up. "Rachel and Ruby, let's take a look at the
farm," he suggested. The three walked out the back door, leaving Hildy and her stepmother alone with their arms about each
other. As they talked things through, Hildy felt enclosed in a
warm cocoon, and her anger dissolved.

Suddenly a man's voice interrupted them from outside the
open parlor window. "Anybody home?"

Hildy spun toward the window. "Daddy?"

"Joe!" Molly exclaimed.

Hildy leaped up and ran to the window. Bending close to the
wire screen, she looked out. "Daddy!"

Joe Corrigan's clothes were rumpled, and he needed a shave.
His blue eyes were bloodshot, and weariness showed in his
deeply tanned face, but his smile was wide and warm.

"My two favorite women!" he cried, sweeping off his wide-
brimmed cowboy hat to press his face against the screen.

With a joyous whoop, Hildy bolted from the room and ran
outside, with Molly right behind.

Joe rushed toward them and crushed them in a mighty bear
hug. His stubbly black beard scratched Hildy's cheeks, but she
didn't care. "You're here!" she cried. "You're here!"

"Yes," he whispered, kissing both Molly and Hildy again
and again. "I'm here. Where're the rest of the kids?"

"They're with my parents in Foleyville," Molly explained.
"They'll be back soon."

Joe blinked and stared at his daughter. "Hildy, you've been
crying? What happened?"

"It's a long story. I'll tell you later. Come on, Daddy, tell us
about California."

All three of them talked at once, babbling away with questions and sudden thoughts as they headed for the back porch.
Just then Seth, Rachel, and Ruby came running in from the silo.

After some brief introductions, Hildy's father explained his
situation. "I've only got a few days to get back or I lose my job,"
he told them soberly. "I drove day and night getting here. Slept

a little in the car when I had to, just to make good time. But it just about tore up that poor old Essex car of mine. We've got to get started back, but first I've got to try selling the Essex. Right now, it'll only go about twenty-five miles an hour, and that's if it's downhill and there's a good tail wind."

He winked at Hildy. "I'm a pretty fair mechanic, but I don't think that old shoe box with wheels can get us all to California on time. So I'm hoping I can sell the Essex for enough that along with the little bit of savings I've got, I can buy some train tickets for all of us."

"We're going to ride the train?" She turned wide-eyed to Ruby and they hugged each other excitedly.

"We will if I can sell that Essex," her father replied. "But I'd better get into town and see if I can find a buyer."

"We have to leave right away then?" Molly asked.

Joe Corrigan nodded. "Yes. You'd better pack. Soon's the kids get here, we can start. Can't afford to lose my job!"

Hildy frowned. "What a mean ol' boss you must have."

"Don't blame him. He's tough, all right, but he's got ranch work that needs to be done every day. There are a hundred men anxious to do it because times are so hard. So I can understand why he said I've got to be back in time or he'll give my job to someone else. Besides, he's got a house we can live in, rent free, while I work for him. So let's save our talking for later and get busy," he finished with a grin.

Molly smiled up at her husband. "I'm all packed except for what the kids needed today. Soon's they get back with my parents, we can be on our way."

"Good," Joe replied. "Folks," he said, turning to Seth and Rachel, "if you'll excuse me, I've got to drive into Foleyville and try selling my heap. If we want to get to California in time, we have to catch the train by five o'clock this afternoon!"

"Daddy," Hildy pleaded, "it's okay if Ruby goes to California with us, isn't it?"

He frowned. "Two adults and five kids is going to be pretty expensive, but Molly, you can probably use some help with the kids on such a long train ride—'specially the baby—can't you?"

"I'll need both girls," Molly agreed.

"Then it's settled," Joe agreed.

Hildy and Ruby gave each other another quick hug.

Joe Corrigan turned to Seth and Rachel. "I hope you understand."

"We shore do," Seth replied, reaching out and taking his bride's hand. "Well, reckon we'uns better be a-gittin' along toward Chicago, anyway."

Everyone said goodbye to the newlyweds, but only Hildy and Ruby walked outside to the roofless Model T with them. Next to Seth's car sat Joe Corrigan's square black car, muddy and covered with road grime.

"Goodbye, Seth. Goodbye, Rachel," Ruby said solemnly. "I'm proud to know ye both. I hope ye have a happy life together." She hesitated, then suddenly reached out to hug them.

Hildy also gave them warm hugs. "I'll never forget what you two did for us," she murmured.

Seth smiled down on her. "Rachel'n me'll both feel better, knowin' yore pa is with ye gals, an' Vester won't bother ye no more."

Hildy had forgotten their pursuer for the moment. She wondered briefly where he was, then shook off the thought. It didn't matter anymore. Dad was here now and Vester wouldn't dare come close. In about three hours, they'd be taking a train out of Illinois, and Vester would be out of their lives forever.

The cousins stood under the shady maple trees, waving at Seth and Rachel until the Model T turned into the lane. Then Hildy's father came out of the house, and the girls talked him into letting them ride into Foleyville with him.

Hildy didn't know anything about cars, but the way the Essex missed and backfired, Hildy hoped her father would be able to get enough money out of it for their train tickets. They definitely needed something better. The idea of driving that car twenty-five hundred miles scared her.

At the edge of town, they bumped across double railroad tracks, and headed toward the middle of Foleyville. Hildy heard a distant train whistle as the Essex labored past the railroad yards onto the town's main cobblestone street.

For an hour, the girls trailed Mr. Corrigan while he went around to the few car dealers in town. Nobody wanted to buy the Essex, and soon Mr. Corrigan began to get impatient.

"Well, there's one more possibility," he remarked. "I'll try that Chevy place near the train depot, the one we passed coming into town."

He drove back across the double tracks that ran along the eastern edge of Foleyville. There were only vacant lots on one side of the street except for the Chevrolet dealer. A row of small shops stood across the street, but almost all of them were boarded up. The Depression kept most people from buying anything but absolute necessities.

Mr. Corrigan parked the grimy Essex half a block away from the car dealer. "Don't want to lose the sale before I get started," he explained with a grin.

Hildy studied the row of cars lined up outside the showroom window. Most were used. There wasn't much market for new cars.

"Now those look mighty nice," her father said with forced cheerfulness as they approached. "Let's see what luck we have here."

Ruby nudged Hildy with an elbow. "Hey! Lookee thar acrost the street. That's a real dress shop."

Father and daughter glanced past a horse and buggy going by, followed by a car that looked a little bit like Seth's.

Ruby was exuberant. "I ain't never seen brand new dresses afore, Hildy. Let's go look."

Hildy glanced at her father.

He nodded. "Look all you want. Just remember, our family's future depends on us all getting back to Lone River before my boss gives my job away. We can't miss that five o'clock train."

Hildy nodded. "Meet you here?"

"No. I might try to sell the car somewhere else. Meet me at the train depot. See it?" he said, pointing, then swung his arm toward the center of town. "See the clock on top of that bank building? Keep an eye on it. You've got to be at the train depot by five o'clock sharp!"

"We'll be back on time," both girls promised.

Hildy and Ruby dashed across the cobblestone street, dodging horses and automobiles, then stopped and peered through the window at dresses. The most either had ever owned at once were two used dresses—a Sunday one and an everyday one.

After a few minutes of excited comments about the riches in the windows, Ruby tugged at Hildy's arm. "Come on. Let's look in some more winders."

"I don't know," Hildy said uneasily. "We shouldn't get too far away from Daddy."

"Oh, stop worrying." Ruby pointed across an alley. "There's another shop. Let's take a look."

As they stepped off the high curb, a square, green, closed sedan suddenly shot out from the alley and stopped beside them.

"What—?" Hildy exclaimed.

She and Ruby jumped back in surprise as the driver leaped out, leaving his door open. He reached back, jerked the rear door open and spun toward the girls.

"Vester!" Hildy cried.

"Git in!" The red-bearded, pock-faced moonshiner reached out and grabbed each girl by the arm.

"Let go!" Hildy cried, striking with her free hand at the iron grip on her forearm.

Ruby fought back, too, but Vester was too strong. In seconds, they were dumped like sacks of potatoes into the backseat. The door slammed, and the car raced down the cobblestone street out of town.

Chapter Nineteen

WHEN TIME RUNS OUT

Fifteen minutes later, both girls had been dumped into the corner of an abandoned railroad car. The dirty cattle car sat at the far end of a spur track, weeds growing high about it.

Hildy quickly scanned their surroundings. Except for some yellow straw on the floor, the car was empty. The heavy side slats let in air and filtered light, but the smell of the car's former occupants was strong.

Hildy trembled with fear as Vester tied up Ruby, then bound Hildy's hands behind her back and tied her ankles with Manila rope. "By the way, yellin' won't do no good," he told the girls. "We'uns is plumb back at the far end of the railroad yards. Noise of trains goin' by'll keep ye from bein' heard. Anyways, ain't nobody likely to come 'round here."

Hildy tried to hide her fear by bluffing. "You'd better let us go! My father's trying to sell his car just down the street, and he's expecting us back in a few minutes."

Vester gave the rope an extra hard pull so that it cut into Hildy's wrists crossed behind her back. "I know all about yore ol' man, jist like I knowed ye'd come to Foleyville. Think yore so smart!"

Ruby kicked her unbound feet against Vester's legs. "Wait'll we git free, Vester Hardesty!" she yelled. "Y'all go to jail fer-ever!"

Vester laughed. "That's whar yore wrong, girlie—jist like y'all was wrong 'bout ever'thin' else. Ye didn't know I could drive a car, did ye? I learnt a few years back. Same time I rode the rods on freight trains like this'n. I went most ever'place them days, includin' this yard."

Hildy made herself look straight into her captor's eyes. "My daddy'll get you for this!"

"That don't bother me none, Hildy. I been a-watchin' him tryin' to sell that ol' wreck of a car. He won't know where to look fer ye. Come nightfall, nobody'll find either of ye."

Hildy's spirits sagged. An hour earlier, everything seemed to be going great. Now her world was coming apart again. And once again, she felt the need for strength and wisdom greater than her own.

Vester stood back and looked at both girls. He was obviously pleased with himself. "I'm smarter'n ye give me credit fer. Like back there on the road. Y'all thought lettin' the air outta my tahrs would stop me."

He laughed a low, evil laugh. "Well, some farmer stopped to he'p me, and I done stole his car, same's the first one. Came straight here, 'cause Granny Dunnigan tol' me 'bout Molly's parents livin' outside'a town. That old crow tol' me 'bout the place in Oklahoma, too. They's no way ye two could git away from me!"

He turned to Ruby, his hard eyes glittering. "That o'nery ol' granny woman said I was'ta bring Hildy back without hurtin' her or she'd skin me alive. But she didn't say nothin' 'bout bein' nice to *you*, Ruby, my purty one."

Ruby crouched in the dry yellow straw in the corner of the car. Her upper lip drew back from the right corner of her mouth, showing teeth like a cornered animal. "Tetch me an' I'll whup ye so hard y'all land clean back acrost the Mississippi!"

Vester laughed again, stroking his untidy beard. "Li'l wild-cat, ain't ye? Or mebby yore more like a flower bud 'bout to bloom, not like yore skinny cousin thar. But first, let's git yore feet tied, too."

He reached for Ruby with a piece of Manila rope trailing from his big hand. Ruby leaped from her crouching position, heading for the sliding door, which stood slightly open in the middle of the boxcar. As Vester swerved to catch her, Ruby dodged to the left and dashed for the open door on the opposite side of the car.

For a heavyset man, Vester was surprisingly quick. Grabbing Ruby's bound arms, he swung her hard against the slatted car walls. She groaned and fell. Before she could move, Vester knotted the rope around her ankles, snugging them tightly together.

"Now then," he said with satisfaction. "Reckon that'll hold ye both whilst I git rid of that stolen car. Likely someone saw me grab y'all, so the law'll be a-lookin' fer it. Be right back, so don't go 'way!" He laughed at his own humor and slipped out of the cattle car.

Hildy watched through the slats as their captor cautiously dodged from one railroad spur to another, taking cover behind the empty cars. Within moments he disappeared.

Hildy turned anxious eyes to Ruby. "You hurt?"

"Naw! Kinda knocked the wind outta me fer a secont, though."

"We've got to get out of here!" Hildy exclaimed, struggling against her bonds. "Daddy'll have to leave without us if we're not back in time."

Through the slats and across the railroad yard with its lines of motionless cars, Hildy saw a long freight train. As it rumbled through the railroad yard, the powerful steam engine poured black coal smoke into the air. The bell clanged and the whistle sounded a warning for the depot street crossing.

Hildy's eyes lifted to the town clock on top of the bank building. The clock hands indicated twenty minutes past two. Hildy groaned. "We've only got two hours and forty minutes!"

Ruby struggled to get out of her own ropes. "Aw, yore pa won't leave without ye," she protested.

"What else could he do? If he loses his job, we're all in trouble. And he doesn't know about Vester. Neither does Molly. So after he finds a buyer for his car, he'll go get Molly and the kids, finish off the deal, and walk over to the train depot. Trains don't wait for people. We have to be there at five o'clock, no matter what!"

"Come on, then!" Ruby cried. "Let's get these ropes untied before Vester comes back."

Both girls struggled mightily, but the strong ropes would not yield.

Perspiration began to form on Hildy's forehead as she heard footsteps along the abandoned railroad tracks. She stopped struggling and listened hopefully, ready to cry out for help.

Ruby raised up and peered through the corner slat. "It's him! He's back!"

Both girls sagged wearily against the smelly straw. Hildy glanced at the tower clock. It read 2:55.

Their captor opened the heavy sliding door and crawled in. "I left that car in a field of ol' wagons and junk," he announced. "Nobody saw me, so now we jist got to wait fer dark. Then I'll swipe another car, and we're off to the Ozarks."

He reached into his overall pocket and produced a plug of chewing tobacco. Studying both girls with hard eyes, he dug a heavy jackknife from another pocket, opened it and cut off a chunk of tobacco. Then he put the tobacco in his mouth and began chewing.

Hildy looked away in disgust as a trickle of brown juice trailed from the corner of his mouth and down his bearded chin. Vester didn't seem to notice. He placed the back end of the knife blade against his overall-clad leg and closed it halfway.

Suddenly he stopped, the back of the blade still against his leg. "Listen!" he hissed, dropping the knife. It fell almost silently into the straw on the floor.

Hildy strained to hear. "Men's voices," she whispered to Ruby. "Coming this way."

Vester took a few quick steps to the door and peered through the slats. Then he spun around, yanking a crumpled red and white polka-dot handkerchief from his hip pocket.

"Railroad bulls," he muttered, tearing the cloth in two. "I shoulda knowed they'd check ever'thin' in the yards on reg'lar patrol."

Hildy had never heard of "railroad bulls," but she guessed they were security guards for railroad property. She opened her mouth to scream.

Immediately Vester leaped forward and jammed one piece of the handkerchief into her mouth. It smelled of chewing tobacco, and Hildy gagged.

Vester swung toward Ruby and pulled the other piece of cloth tightly about her mouth. "If'n either of ye so much as lets out a peep, ye won't have time to say a prayer!" he whispered hoarsely. "I won't be here when the bulls come, an' by then it'll be too late fer both of ye!"

He shoved the girls into the straw and warned them not to move. Then running quietly to the far end of the car, he flopped onto the floor and watched the approaching men.

Hildy heard them sliding boxcar doors open. *They're opening every car and checking to see that no hobos are inside*, she thought. *They'll do the same here.*

Her heart soared with hope, then plunged in despair. *If they start to open one of the doors on this car, Vester will escape out the other. But . . . what'll he do to us first?* She remembered his threat and shivered.

Hildy turned desperately toward her cousin, trying to communicate with her eyes that help was coming . . . if only they could alert the security guards.

But how? Both girls' hands were tied behind their backs with Manila rope. And their feet, bound at the ankles, stuck straight out in front of them on the straw.

All of a sudden Hildy had an idea. Her eyes met Ruby's; then she jerked her head toward her bound feet. Silently lifting them from the straw, she lowered them again, suggesting that both girls kick on the floor and make noise.

Ruby glanced at the straw and shook her head. Hildy frowned, but soon realized what Ruby meant. The straw wasn't more than a few inches thick, but it would deaden the sound of their kicking.

Hildy lifted her gaze through the slats to the clock tower. *Two minutes after three*, she thought. *Less than two hours! If we could just get those men in here fast enough—*

The jackknife! She interrupted her own thoughts.

Her eyes shot to the straw near her outstretched feet. *Vester dropped his jackknife in the straw after cutting his plug of tobacco. But where?* Not able to see the knife, she began cautiously moving her heels through the straw. *It's got to be right around—there!* she thought.

Gingerly lowering her feet, she found the knife, still half open. She started to pull her knees up, dragging the knife through the straw toward her, then stopped. She glanced fearfully at Vester, who was flat on his stomach, watching the approaching men through the car slats.

Hildy could also see them now. There were two of them—big, burly men, each armed with some kind of heavy club. Although still some distance away, they were methodically moving closer, checking each car.

Vester slid backward until he was even with the doors, then turned around. Instantly, Hildy stopped pulling the partially buried knife toward her.

Vester stood up. "Cain't let 'em look in here, can we?" he asked quietly. "Ye ever see a fox lead the houn' dawgs away from his den?"

Hildy didn't understand. She glanced at Ruby, whose furrowed brow showed she didn't either. Hildy looked up at Vester again.

But soon he sank into a crouching position, watching the men, who were now nearing the far end of three boxcars coupled together. There was a space of about a hundred yards between the nearest of the three boxcars and the cattle car. Both men walked along the right side of the tracks as they left the far car and started for the next.

Vester eased to the left side of the car and stood up, poised by the partly open door. He turned to grin at the girls. "Soon's them bulls git right smack dab in the middle so's it'll be harder fer them to git 'round the cars . . . Now!"

Leaping out of the left side of the car, he landed in a crouched position, regained his feet, and started running past silent coal cars, gondolas, and boxcars.

"Hey, you! Stop!" the guards shouted. Then there was the sound of running feet.

Hildy watched through the slats as the two railroad men sprinted beside the middle boxcar. It would take them precious seconds to reach the end of the three-car string where they could chase the fleeing Vester unhindered.

Hildy wanted to watch, but this was her chance to escape. She glanced at the tower clock: 3:15.

She dragged her feet toward her, the knife sliding with them. When it was close to where she was sitting, she gingerly scraped the straw away.

The knife glittered brightly in a ray of sunshine.

Hildy shot a look at Ruby, whose eyes were open wide in understanding. Hildy looked back down at the knife and began inching her body sideways, bringing her bound hands closer to the half-open blade.

Got it! she told herself triumphantly as her fingers closed around the handle. Signalling with her eyes, she mumbled excitedly against her gag, hoping Ruby would understand.

Hildy eased the blade upward, but stopped in dismay as the blade cut her wrist slightly. She gripped the knife carefully, lowered the blade through the straw to the floor, and cautiously pressed until she felt the blade snap to a fully open position.

Scooting across the boxcar to Ruby, she mumbled through her gag, "I can't cut my own ropes. Let me try yours."

Ruby took a moment to understand, then hurriedly turned her back and hitched her body close to touch her cousin's hands.

Gingerly, Hildy eased the blade up until she felt it rest against Ruby's ropes. Very carefully, Hildy began sawing away, but the knife didn't seem to be cutting well. Minutes slid away, and Hildy glanced at the town clock.

Three thirty? she thought. *Oh, Lord! Keep Vester away long enough for us to get free!*

Perspiration rolled down Hildy's face as she continued working with the knife. It was hard to cut so slowly and carefully with her hands behind her back. She could not see what she was doing. Occasionally, she felt Ruby flinch and knew the knife had drawn blood. Still, Hildy worked on, glancing up every once in a while at the clock as time move steadily on.

Two minutes of four! That can't be right! she thought.

Ruby's bonds still held.

Ruby mumbled something through her gag and shoved against her cousin's shoulder.

Hildy stopped cutting and listened. *Vester! He's coming back!* she thought, seeing him a long way off, across the railroad yard. He was in no hurry. Obviously, he had lost his pursuers.

Ruby made a strangled sound through her gag, and Hildy understood that her cousin meant "Hurry!"

Hildy took a chance and cut harder. Soon she felt Ruby's rope start to separate. *Oh, Lord,* she prayed in anguish, *help us, please!*

It was five minutes after four when Ruby's ropes parted and fell away. With her hands free, Ruby immediately yanked off her gag, and then Hildy's.

Quickly Ruby snatched the knife from Hildy. "Hold still," she whispered. "I'm gonna cut fast."

As Hildy felt the blade sliding rapidly between her wrists, she shot a fearful glance through the slats. Vester was within a hundred yards. "Hurry! Hurry!" Hildy cried. The clock read ten after four when Hildy felt her ropes snap apart. Rubbing her raw wrists, she turned to face Ruby, who reached down and began cutting her own ankle ropes.

"Faster!" Hildy urged, stretching her ankles out for her ropes to be cut next. "Faster!"

"I cain't go no faster with this dull knife."

But in less than a minute Ruby's ankles were free, and she immediately started sawing across Hildy's ankle bonds. Soon they, too, fell off.

Both girls started to jump up, then stopped. Vester was humming to himself, walking along the left side of the cattle car. The door was still open where he'd jumped out, but the other one was closed.

Hildy glanced around, desperately trying to decide what to do. The girls certainly couldn't outrun Vester unless they had a head start. He was probably a little tired after running away from the railroad men, but he was a mountaineer and hunter. It took tremendous physical stamina to follow hunting dogs night after night, and Vester was a master at that.

"Too late!" Hildy said in a hoarse whisper. "Hide the gag and your ropes in the straw. Bury your ankles, and put your hands behind your back again."

Hildy sat down abruptly and shoved her feet into the straw, hiding the cut ropes. She put her hands behind her back as Ruby did the same. Hildy wished there were time to put the gags back, but Vester was too close.

Vester climbed through the open sliding door. "I reckon now nobody'll bother us, an' then when it's dark we kin start south." He walked across the straw to peer down at his captives. "Well, long's we got to wait a spell yet, may's well—"

He stopped suddenly, his eyes clouding with suspicion. "Hey! How'd y'all git them gags off?"

"We spit 'em out 'cause they was so filthy an' ye didn't tie 'em that tight!" Ruby said quickly.

Vester considered her explanation for a moment, then nodded. "Maybe I didn't tie 'em right. Oh, well, y'all didn't screech, so we may's well leave 'em off so's we kin talk."

He pulled the plug of chewing tobacco from his pocket again. "Reckon I'll jist have me another chaw. Then I'd best check yore ropes agin. Now, whar'd I put my knife?"

Hildy and Ruby exchanged fearful glances as Vester felt around in his pocket. Hildy's eyes peered through the slats at the distant clock. *Only twenty minutes left!*

CHAPTER TWENTY

LAST DESPERATE TRY

Vester patted his pockets harder. "Now, whar's my knife?"

Hildy heard another distant train whistle. She had been hearing them for the last couple of hours, but suddenly a daring idea popped into her head. It was risky, but it offered the only hope. "I want a drink," she blurted out.

Ruby stared at her in total surprise.

Vester stuck his hand into his overall pocket again, feeling for the knife. "Ye don't need nothin'."

"You want me to tell Granny you wouldn't give me something to drink when I was dying of thirst?"

"That ol' granny woman don't scare me none."

Hildy listened to the train drawing closer, her mind spinning like the engine's great drive wheels. A lonesome whistle sounded, then another. It was almost like an echo but from different directions.

Hildy pretended not to care what Vester did but played on his superstitious nature. "Well, Granny won't put no spells on me, but *you*—"

"Ain't no sech things!" the mountaineer said without conviction. He stopped looking for his knife and nervously fingered his rabbit's foot on a chain.

Ruby gave Hildy a knowing look. "I say they is," she said fervently. "Haints is real. So's the spells that granny woman kin put on the likes of *you*, Vester."

Hildy had never heard of her grandmother casting spells as some old mountain women did, but maybe Vester didn't know that. And Ruby could be convincing because she, like many mountain folk, had an unreasonable fear of "haunts."

Hildy became bolder. "I wonder what it's like to go through life with a haunt bothering a person because he wouldn't give a girl a drink of water," she mused.

Vester seemed to forget about the knife. "Ain't no drinkin' water 'round here," he growled.

"Then get me a soda pop. Must be one in a store close by."

Ruby seemed to be understanding her cousin's actions more and more. "Better get her some sody water afore the stores close. See that clock yonder? Comin' up on five o'clock—closin' time fer some places, ain't it?"

Vester swore under his breath. Releasing the rabbit's foot, he stomped over to the open sliding door and glanced around to make sure nobody was watching. Then he jumped down.

Hildy stood up and held her breath as she watched Vester hurrying across the railroad yard. He darted from the shelter of one car to another, obviously watching for the security men.

Ruby looked up at her cousin. "What're ye doin'?" she whispered.

"Shhh! Come on." Hildy led the way to the open sliding door. "Soon as he gets out of sight past that next car, get ready to run the opposite direction."

"Let's wait till he's clean out of the yard."

"There's no time to wait. Look at the clock!"

"But Vester kin outrun us!"

"Not if the good Lord helps us," Hildy told her. "Hear that train?"

"Sounds like two."

"I just hear one, but that doesn't matter. If we can time it right, we can run across the tracks just before that engine gets there."

"Then Vester'll be cut off." Ruby clapped her hands joyfully and leaped to her feet. "And we can run to meet yore pa."

"Let's hope it's a long freight train instead of a short one. That'd give us even more time before Vester could cross after us."

Hildy glanced at the distant clock. "Only ten minutes left, and it's a long way to the depot. If we're not there by the time my father leaves, Vester'll catch us again! This is our only chance. You ready?"

"Ready."

"Let's go!"

The girls sat down on their backsides and shoved themselves out the sliding door from the high train bed. Landing hard on their feet, they staggered, then recovered their balance. Hildy stole a quick look toward Vester. He was still sneaking the other way across the railroad yards.

The girls raced hard toward the main line of railroad tracks and the approaching freight train.

They had only covered a few yards when Vester started yelling, "Hey! Stop!" His shouts became lost in the locomotive's whistle.

Hildy glanced back only long enough to see Vester start running across the railroad yards toward them. He was surprisingly fast for a big man.

"Faster!" Hildy cried.

Ruby was pacing her cousin, arms pumping, across the yards. "I am! I am!"

Vester's voice sounded closer. "Stop, I said!"

Hildy stole a quick look back and moaned. "He's gaining fast!"

Ruby glanced back to see for herself. "Shore is! We'll never make it!"

"We've got to. The train's almost here."

"He's gonna ketch us shore." Ruby's voice broke.

"If he gets too close, we split up. You go right. I'll go left. Meet at the train depot."

"Vester'll chase after ye, Hildy. He thinks Granny's gonna

put a spell on him. He's gotta git ye!"

"If he does, try to reach my father. Call a guard. Do something. But keep running!"

Ruby was breathing hard, her words jarred by the constant leaping over railroad ties and dodging old boxcars. "I'm gonna stop an' delay him. You call fer help and then go on to Californy with yore family."

"No! No! Please, Ruby. Keep running. We're almost there."

Ruby wordlessly obeyed. The cousins raced toward the oncoming freight train, but both girls were starting to tire. They staggered, sucking air in great, ragged gulps. The mighty steam locomotive, its bell clanging and whistle screaming, hurtled toward the spot where the girls had to cross the tracks.

Hildy thought the rail bed looked unusually wide, but that didn't matter. All she had to do was beat the train across the tracks to be safe.

"Don't do anything foolish," she called aloud, glancing back. Vester was closing fast. "If we see we can't make it safely, we'd better stop. We're better off with Vester than getting hit by a train!"

"I'm not so shore of that!" Ruby exclaimed.

Hildy took one final look down the tracks at the thundering approach of the steam engine. Then she almost smiled. "We've got plenty of time!" she shouted. "Careful! Don't fall when you run across the tracks!"

The train's whistle split the afternoon air with a long, warning blast.

Hildy glanced fearfully at the massive locomotive screaming toward them. "Oh, Lord," she panted as her feet hit the graveled railroad bed, "help us!"

Reaching the main line together, the girls leaped the first iron rail and landed in the middle of the black railroad ties. Without stopping they jumped to clear the second rail.

Hildy stumbled and started to fall in the middle of the tracks.

The whistle sounded long and loud, and Hildy fell forward. Tripping over the second rail, she landed on her hands and knees in the gravel just beyond the glistening rail.

The train rumbled past with its whistle screaming.

"Ruby?" Hildy cried fearfully, turning around.

Panting but smiling, Ruby reached down and helped Hildy up. "We's made it!" Ruby cried over the noise of the passing train. She threw her arms around her cousin.

"And Vester didn't!" Hildy exclaimed, breathing hard.

Exhausted from their all-out, frantic run, Hildy and Ruby bent down and peered between the iron wheels flashing past. They could see Vester's legs stomping up and down on the other side of the passing train.

"He's mighty sore," Ruby said hoarsely, gasping for breath.

As the freight train cars clacked by on the steel rails, Hildy glanced up at the clock.

"Five minutes!" she gasped. "Come on. We've barely got time—"

"Wait!" Ruby grabbed Hildy's arm frantically. "Look!"

Suddenly Hildy saw a second locomotive bearing down on them from the opposite direction. Too late, she remembered the wide rail bed—this was the main freight line, and there were actually two sets of tracks not more than a few feet apart!

There was no time to run across the next tracks. The second freight train was upon them in a thunder of drive wheels and a blasting whistle. The girls were trapped between two trains going opposite directions.

"Get down!" Hildy shouted above the roar. "Lie down flat right here. Pull your hands close to your body, and keep your feet together!"

She wasn't sure Ruby could hear, so she demonstrated by dropping flat on her stomach in the gravel and cinders separating the two sets of tracks. Ruby immediately did the same. As the ground trembled beneath them, both girls instinctively covered their heads with their arms.

For about a minute, the trains continued to roar past, each headed a different direction. Then a terrible thought hit Hildy.

Raising her head slightly, she shouted in Ruby's ear just inches away. "If the first train passes before the other one, we'll be cut off, but Vester can get to us!"

Ruby's eyes widened. She and Hildy turned to look through the flashing wheels of the first train. Vester was crouched down, watching them, and Hildy was sure he had thought of the same thing.

Which train'll finish passing first? The thought seared through Hildy's mind.

There was nothing she could do—nothing anybody could do—but wait. She raised anxious eyes to the town clock. *One minute to five.*

In that moment, Hildy knew the turnaround in her life was complete. She belonged to God now. Her lips moved silently. "Oh, Lord, no matter what happens, when we get out of here, I'm going to be with you always."

She glanced at Ruby and was surprised to see that her lips were also moving in silent prayer.

A quick look at the town clock showed exactly five o'clock. Hildy groaned, but the two trains kept rushing by at a steady speed.

Another minute passed. Two. Three. Four . . . *Maybe our train'll be late,* she thought hopefully.

Hildy tore her eyes off the clock as the noise of the trains seemed to change slightly. Hildy looked up. "Oh, no!" she cried in disbelief.

The caboose of the first train charged quickly toward them. Its red light on the side glowed like a final warning of what was to come.

Hildy grabbed Ruby's arm and pointed. Both girls, flat on their stomachs, watched in fearful fascination as the caboose rattled nearer. Then they glanced through the passing train wheels.

Vester had seen the caboose, too. He grinned and crouched, ready to dash across the tracks and grab the girls the moment the train passed. And they couldn't get away because the second train cut them off from any chance of escape.

In sick despair, Hildy watched the iron rails bounce up and down on the ties as the wheels clicked rhythmically.

Hildy's heart beat wildly as the first caboose swept closer

and closer, faster and faster, with Vester only a few feet away.

Ruby pounded on Hildy's shoulder so hard that Hildy almost struck out in self-defense. Ruby was pointing and shouting, but Hildy couldn't hear a word. Hildy looked behind them, where her cousin was pointing.

The second train was still rumbling by, but it was a shorter one, and its caboose was also coming up fast. But would it go by before the other one let Vester catch the girls?

Hildy raised her eyes to the late afternoon sky. "Oh, please, let this one pass first!" she cried.

Hildy got to her knees, then crouched, ready to run. Out of the corner of her eye, she saw Ruby do the same. Above the thunderous roar of the passing trains, Hildy yelled, "A few more seconds . . ."

The instant the second train's caboose passed, both girls leaped up. Rushing over the extra set of tracks, they quickly dashed the few feet to the cobblestone street, then raced toward the depot.

"Too late!" Ruby cried as they reached the platform. "Look at the clock. It's six minutes after five. They're already gone!"

"Maybe not! Let's go ask!"

Hurrying inside the depot building, Hildy's anxious eyes searched for someone who could help. Seeing a young, dark-haired man at the ticket window, she hurried over to him. "Please, sir," she said, out of breath, "can you tell me if the five o'clock train going west left on time?"

"Why, yes! Our trains always run on time," the young man replied. Then he frowned at the sight of her stricken face and asked, "Is there anything I can do for you?"

"Did a man and woman with four little girls and a baby get on board?"

The dark-haired young man shook his head. "An old man and a woman got off, but no one got on. Not many people traveling by train these days."

Hildy took a deep breath and turned to Ruby. "Maybe Daddy couldn't sell the car! Come on! Let's look outside!"

As the two girls turned, Hildy glanced out the grimy depot

window back the way they'd come. Both trains had passed, and Vester was running hard toward the depot. Hildy pointed. "He's coming! Quick! Out the other door!"

They dashed across the empty waiting room with its smell of stale cigar smoke. Hildy jerked open the far door and ran outside, Ruby right behind her.

Both girls spun around to look back. Vester was out of sight, but it was only a matter of time until he found them again. Hildy frantically looked around.

To the left, empty railroad tracks showed where the five o'clock passenger train had passed. Straight ahead, in a vacant lot, there were only a couple of automobiles and three wagons, but no people.

Hildy glanced to the right. A horse and buggy crunched gravel as an older couple and a gray-haired driver turned from the depot onto the cobblestone street.

"Come on!" Ruby cried. "Ain't no use a-standin' here a-lookin'! Nobody in sight kin he'p us!"

"Maybe Daddy's parked at the curb in front of the depot!" Hildy replied hopefully, starting to run in that direction.

As the girls dashed alongside the depot wall, Ruby glanced through a window as they passed. "Vester's inside an' a-comin' this way!"

Hildy's desperate glance over her shoulder proved that Ruby was right.

The girls continued to run toward the curb. Ruby puffed, "I don't see yore family anywheres! An' I've got a turrible stitch in my side! We'uns may's well give up!"

Hildy's own lungs burned and her side ached, but she couldn't quit. She couldn't let her cousin stop, either. "If you want a chance to maybe someday find your father, keep running!"

Ruby groaned. "Yore right! I'm gonna keep a-goin'! Hey! Lookee!" she shouted as they rounded the depot corner nearest the cobblestone street.

Hildy's hopes surged. To the right, nearer town, the Essex bounced down the street toward them!

"Daddy!" Hildy shouted.

In their excitement both girls found new strength to run toward the oncoming car piled full of kids and belongings. Four towheaded little girls stuck their heads out the open sides and waved wildly.

Joe Corrigan cut the front wheels sharply toward the high curb. He yanked back hard on the hand brake and leaped out of the driver's seat as the girls collapsed against him.

"Oh, Daddy! Daddy!" Hildy whispered as he gathered both runners in his strong arms and hugged them.

He whispered against Hildy's hair, "Sorry we're late, but it took longer to get ready than I thought. You two look all tuckered out! You both okay?"

Ruby cried, "Y'all won't believe what's happened since we'uns left ye a while ago! Vester—!"

"Vester!" Hildy interrupted, spinning around to see where their relentless pursuer was.

He was halfway between the depot and the curb and skidding to a stop just as a police car pulled up. Vester turned and dashed back toward the depot. The uniformed officer leaped from the patrol unit and chased after Vester.

Ruby clapped her hands and yelled, "Git him, Mister Policeman! Git him good!"

The officer caught up to the mountaineer just as he tried to escape through the side depot door.

Joe Corrigan, concerned, asked, "What's all that about?"

"Tell you later, Daddy!" Hildy turned her face upward and whispered, "Thanks for everything!"

"Well," her father said, "I'm sure glad we found you two girls!"

"You wouldn't believe how glad we are to see you!" Hildy exclaimed. She added, "You couldn't sell the Essex, huh?"

"No," he replied. "You girls run around the other side and slide into the backseat. This side's piled too high with stuff."

As the happy cousins ran around the back of the Essex, Hildy noticed a crudely printed sign on the spare tire cover: "CALI-

FORNIA OR BUST!" That looked like the work of her ten-year-old sister, Elizabeth.

Laughing with joy and relief, Hildy and Ruby piled into the backseat where they were engulfed into eager arms of four little girls.

As Mr. Corrigan slid back under the wheel, he remarked, "Since I couldn't sell the car, I'm trusting it'll get us to California on time!"

Hildy breathed a sigh of relief. "Just thank the Lord we all found each other again!"

Molly shifted the sleepy baby Joey in her arms and twisted to reach across the front seat and grip Hildy's arm. "Amen to that," she agreed.

Hildy threw her arms wide and gathered all of her sisters and Ruby together. "Next stop," she shouted joyfully, "our 'forever' home!"

A chorus of joyful cheers echoed her words as the car headed west toward California.